Twice Upon a Time in Fairyland

Laurie Lee

ISBN: 978-1-962168-07-6

Wolf and the Girl with the

Red Cloak

This tale is based on the collection of stories well known as Little Red Riding Hood. There are both French and German roots to the original fairytale. The earliest publication may have been by Perrault, where innocence clashes with evil. Oral tellings of Red Riding Hood are much older, often more gruesome, and darker than we normally think of fairytales in our modern age. This twisting of the tale is also dark, a caution of the evils of greed, or perhaps the dangers of mental illness untreated.

This retelling involves peril and the use of spells to control and manipulate circumstances. It may send chills across your neck. It is best read by the fire with a warm mug of hot chocolate.

Chapter 1

S tay on the path," Sorsha Bostich reminded her daughter as she tightened the sash of her cloak.

Crissy cringed. "You tell me the same thing every time."

Sorsha pressed her hand against Crissy's cheek. "And every time you return safely. I am satisfied."

"I want to go," Sabine declared, peeking around the corner of the kitchen doorway.

Crissy wrinkled her nose at her younger sister. "You are too little. A wolf might gobble you up whole with his afternoon tea."

Sorsha frowned. "No need to fill her head with dark tales."

Crissy smiled at her eight-year-old sibling. "Stay home where you are safe. We will go in a few years."

Sorsha pressed a basket into Crissy's hands. "You best be going. The coin should be enough for a full basket of baked goods."

Crissy kissed her mother's cheek. "Thank you, mother. I will be back before the sun goes down. I may stop and visit Elinor." Crissy skipped through the back door. The midday sun shone brightly overhead, and a cool breeze blew across the garden.

Sabine ran to her side. "Will you bring a cake with cinnamon? Or hard candies? Do you have enough money for that?"

Crissy rolled her eyes. "I will see what fits in the basket."

Sabine twirled. "If you hurry, we can play in the garden. I will be a princess."

Crissy scoffed. "I am the real princess. Hurry back to your dolls before they all disappear."

Sabine scurried away. Crissy watched. Why had mother married another man? Why have another daughter? Life was better when it was just mother and Crissy. She glanced at the half-timber house. Her home. Stepfather and that sweet younger sister were not going to keep her from what was rightfully hers.

She started along the wooded trail. Once she went deep enough not to be seen, she turned aside. She'd already explored most areas but recently crossed a path she'd never noticed before. There hadn't been time that day to go further. Today was a new day. An extraordinary day. She remembered the way well.

She paused when she reached the narrow path. Perhaps an animal made the trail, and yet, something about it caused her skin to tingle. Beneath twisting oaks grew holly bushes and wild roses. For what did she wait? Curiosity drove her onward. Brambles pulled at her cloak, but not enough to stop her from following the dirt path. The branches thickened overhead until it seemed as though she walked within a tunnel. From without, birds called, and insects chatted. But within the tunnel, she was surrounded by a soft hush, as of a breath held before an exhale.

How long she walked, she could not say. It seemed to take hours and hours, and yet, no time at all. Enchantment hovered through the space. The path widened. She heard water running nearby. Something had to be around the bend of the trail. It did not disappoint.

From the tunnel, she stepped into a clearing. Rocks covered in moss dotted the hillside. Thin shafts of light moved like a breeze. There was a flatter area, some of it covered with wildflowers and tangled grasses. Beyond that stood a house wrapped in time's decay. It leaned precariously against a tree trunk.

A wolf's howl caused Crissy to jump. She had come far. Perhaps too far. Light barely reached through the clearing. All she could see beyond the doorway of the house were shadows. She nibbled on her upper lip. "I need to bring a torch."

The sound of her voice stirred the clearing. The tingle in the air should have caused fear. Crissy pressed her hand against her belly. Excitement fluttered. Somewhere inside the house, a lamp lit. She didn't consider running away, but instead moved up the stairs and stepped inside. Her attention was drawn to a dark oak table. A round cloth formed from twists of silk lay on the center of the oblong table. Upon it sat a leather-bound book.

Crissy wrapped the book in the cloth and placed it in the bottom of her basket. The lamp went out.

She half expected the door to slam shut, swallowing her up inside the house. She ran toward the light outside.

Too much time had passed for Crissy to complete her errands. She turned onto the path heading home instead. She'd weave a tale of wolves in the woods, how she tossed food at them to get their attention from herself. Soon, she would be alone in her room, able to explore the book that had been given to her.

~

"You look pale, daughter." Sorsha felt Crissy's forehead.

Crissy almost told her about the book with its strange symbols and lettering. A part of her wanted to tell about the spells. But then *he* walked in.

"How are my girls?" Oleg Bostich's voice boomed as he entered the kitchen. He kissed Crissy on the top of her head, then gathered Sorsha close.

"Papa," Sabine cried as she ran to join them.

Crissy watched him lift her sister. Sabine giggled. Sorsha held his arm. Crissy felt something in her chest twist. It was wrong, but the view displeased her. She wouldn't tell anyone about the book. Instead, she'd hide it away. She somehow knew something within its pages would make the difference she desired.

Chapter 2

Time did not soften Crissy's thoughts towards the usurpers within her home. Sabine grew taller and more lovely. Mother doted on her sweet younger daughter. Crissy drew her red cloak around herself as they prepared to join the May Day festivities in the village.

Sabine skipped around her in the kitchen, soft blooms bouncing in her hair. "I cannot believe I was chosen to weave the May Pole." She stopped and glanced at Crissy. "Did you get to during your fourteenth year?"

She shook her head. "I preferred making a basket and filling it with flowers."

Sabine grinned. "Perhaps today someone will gift you with a basket. Master Johnathan perhaps? Or one of the Torr brothers."

Crissy blushed. Jedison Torr hinted he might try to kiss her as they danced around the May Pole. She shooed Sabine from the house. "Go on. You don't want to be late."

Sabine stood outside the house, gazing at it. Crissy frowned. "Is something wrong?"

She shook her head. "Wondering what it would

be like to put flower boxes beneath the windows."

"It is not your place to make changes."

Sabine laughed. "It is as much mine as yours, silly. Of course, I can make changes." She turned and skipped toward the center of town.

"Too excited to wait for the rest of us?" Sorsha asked as she stepped up behind Crissy.

"I forgot something upstairs. Go on without me, I will catch up." She smiled at Sorsha and Oleg. The pair nodded and walked from the house. Crissy's smile faded away. Anger burned within. How dare Sabine think this house belonged to her? As though she had the right to what Crissy's father had provided. She flounced up the stairs and slammed her door. Something thudded in the small closet. She opened the door and saw the book lying on the floor. She picked it up and went to the window seat where morning light touched the bone-colored pages. She opened somewhere towards the middle, running her fingers over pictures and words. Pages turned, and then something caught her notice. Chills skimmed along her arms as Crissy studied the lines of a spell. She didn't want to kill Sabine, but this could be a way of removing her from the family. At least until Crissy had what she wanted. She settled her back against the wall and read.

~

The month of May passed far too quickly. Memories of weaving the May Pole faded. Something new would take its place. Sabine stood in front of Crissy. "You want me to come with you?"

Crissy chuckled. "I said once you were old

enough. The time has come." She frowned. "Unless you no longer wish to join me."

"Of course, I do," Sabine giggled as she bounced.

"We'll take a basket and enjoy a picnic. I already have a loaf of bread for us." She swung the basket with one hand and linked arms with her sister. "We can stop in town for jam." They left through the kitchen door.

"Shouldn't we be heading that way?" Sabine asked, pausing on the path where it diverged. The path on the left would lead them away from the forest. The other path took them deeper among the trees.

"I prefer a short cut through the forest. Don't worry, it is early in the day. There are no wild creatures to worry about until after dark. We will return long before then."

Sabine nodded. "Then into the woods we go."

It was an easy walk. Sabine closed her eyes and enjoyed the feel of sunlight against her face as she skipped along the path. Crissy strode a few steps ahead. Sabine watched her sister's red cloak flutter through the air as though it was something alive. How many years had she wanted to join Crissy on one of her journeys? Crissy paused and looked back at her. Where Sabine was fair skinned with blonde hair and blue eyes, Crissy had an angular face and thick wavy dark hair. She sighed, oh to be as beautiful as Crissy.

"I have an adventure in mind," Crissy said. "Shall we be explorers? Are you brave, like the men of Spain who set across the ocean?"

Sabine peered around her sister. "Is that a path? Looks more like a trail used by deer."

"Or wolves?" Crissy's eyes widened. "We must be very brave." She chewed on her upper lip.

Sabine took her hand. "I am brave if you are." Though four years separated them in age, Sabine had grown almost as tall as Crissy.

Crissy smiled, and they stepped onto the path. It was as though the sun suddenly turned away from them. Cold crept through her. Crissy released her hand and forged ahead. Sabine took a breath. She needed to be brave, too. Or Crissy might never allow her to join her on a journey again. She followed her sister.

Nary a bird chirped, nor insect hummed through the trees. They'd walked a long time when Sabine slowed her steps. Light splashed across the weathered overhang of an ancient house. "Crissy," she whispered as the hush of the woods settled across her shoulders like a scratchy blanket.

Crissy turned on the path to face her. Sabine pointed. "Who would build a house this deep in the forest?"

Crissy's face brightened. "Grandmother's house." She skipped across a patch of moss.

Sabine shook her head. "We shouldn't be here." Though a chill touched the air, she felt flush, drawn and yet repelled by the Victorian shelter. With its sharp angled roof, the house fit between two great trees. Ornate lintels of deep blue hung beneath the gable, with matching spindles across the porch. Thin clapboards had faded to gray, and moss clung to cracked slate shingles. Present and yet abandoned. A relic of an older age.

Crissy didn't seem to notice. Her eyes shone when she grabbed Sabine's hand. "Grandmother lived here. Not right, that you would find it when she was my grandmother." She squeezed.

Sabine pulled her hand back. "What do you mean, your grandmother? We're sisters. She'd be my grandmother as well." She looked at the house. "And how do you know this is her place? I've never heard of it."

"My grandmother belongs to my father." Crissy tugged her closer to the porch. "Your father didn't have a mother anymore."

Sabine dug her heels into the soft dirt forming a path to the entrance. "Stop it, Crissy. You aren't funny."

But Crissy wouldn't let go. She tugged Sabine to the foot of the stairs. "My father was killed by bandits as he traveled home from a festival far away. Grandmother couldn't bear the news. She died right there, in front of mother and me. Mother dragged me away and we haven't been here since. She moved to town and met your father a year later."

"He's our father, Crissy." Sabine whispered. Her throat tightened. "I don't like this; I want to go home."

"Not yet." The normally calm and fearless Crissy pleaded, her eyes sad. "The house is here. Like I remember it, but older. I had a doll. A tiny thing with blonde hair and porcelain skin." Crissy's eyes filled with tears. Sabine gulped her own, but she couldn't walk away. Crissy pressed her hand.

"Please, Sabine." Her voice was a whisper. "She should be there, if what I remember is true." A single tear dripped from her lashes and coursed down her cheek. "But I can't go in there. Grandmother... but you never knew Grandmother. The house holds no memories for you. Please, Sabine, if you've ever loved me. Please find my doll. At least try."

She didn't want to. Not one ounce of herself wanted to step onto the porch, let alone through the front door that gaped open. The afternoon remained bright, but the forest hid more shadows. She stepped onto the first riser. Her heart quickened, her mind begging her to run in the other direction. But she couldn't, not with Crissy urging her to the next step. Her feet moved, and she stood on the worn boards of the porch, watching dried and shriveled leaves brush across her shoes.

With the door open, she could see into the house. Large windows provided light, so she could make out a tall table, broken chair, and a stone fireplace against a far wall.

"Just a few more steps, Sabine. Please, for me? I promise I won't tease you anymore. You'll be braver than me."

She wasn't brave, but neither could she turn back.

Something changed as she crossed the threshold into the kitchen. The hairs on the back of her neck stood out. Her hand opened and she dropped the willow branch she'd been carrying all morning. Her body tingled, and then waves of pain rolled from her feet, up her legs, through her back, and over her head. She felt as though she bent double, yet she seemed unable to move. Unable to scream though her voice rattled in her throat. Her hands grew larger, longer. Indentations between her knuckles deepened. Her supple skin stretched, brownish spots appearing as its color faded. She stretched a wrinkling hand toward Crissy, but her mind started to gray. Her lips forgot the words pressing against her heart. Weakness pained her legs, and she fell to the stone floor.

~

Crissy held her breath as the air around her shimmered with the working of the spell. Her beautiful, younger sister had changed into an old woman. The force of falling to her feet rippled through heavy flesh. Deep wrinkles marred her face. She could barely see the old woman's eyes.

"Do be careful, Grandmother," Crissy hollered.

Sabine grinned as she waved a gnarled hand. "It's okay, dear. Tell your mother hello. So kind of you to visit."

Crissy walked up the steps and stood in front of the door. "I have a basket of food for you."

"Will you come in?" Sabine's voice wobbled, and she coughed. She still knelt on the floor.

"I mustn't. Just as you must never come out."

Sabine looked at her with faded, milky-blue eyes. Crissy blinked. She placed the basket on the threshold of the door and pushed it toward Sabine with her foot. "Goodbye, Grandmother." A sob scorched her throat. She turned and hurried away.

Sabine's voice followed her. "Goodbye, dear. Oh, I wish I could remember her name."

Crissy ran. The forest enveloped her, and she wiped tears from her cheeks. An hour later, as bells rang through the village, she sat in the middle of the floor of her bedroom, legs crossed, eyes squeezed shut. It was done. *It isn't forever*, she told herself. When the house was hers, and all the things in it, Sabine would be released. Crissy continued to sit until the darkening day made her light a lantern.

The door of her room flew open, banging against the wall. "Have you seen your sister?" Sorsha cried. "She went into the village, but she is long overdue."

Crissy turned. Sorsha's lips were pale, and her hands clutched at a doll with blond hair and blue eyes. "She must be with one of her friends."

"But it is dark outside."

"Have you asked stepfather? Perhaps he should look for her."

The search continued, for days, then weeks, and into months. Crissy huffed as she turned the corner, heading for home after a visit to the village. Someone with a cart waved as he rolled past. Oiled wood peeked through a blanket covering most of the cart. She frowned.

Sorsha stood outside the side door wiping her cheek. Crissy gripped her basket. "What was that?"

Sorsha closed her eyes, then looked at her. "We sold the cabinets from the front room. The mayor has always admired them."

Crissy felt her heart thud. "You sold them? How could you?" She swept past her mother, racing up the steps to the sanctuary of her bedroom. She slammed the door and flung herself across the bed.

Much later, she finally sat up and wiped angry tears from her cheeks. Sabine was gone. Why did they have to fixate on her? Her father had built those cherry oak cabinets. What right did Oleg have to sell them? None. A strangled scream burned her throat. Were they going to sell more of her things? All for the futile search for Sabine? She jerked the book from her closet. It fell from her hands and clattered on the beaten wood floor.

There was a soft knock on the door. Crissy dropped a blanket over the book as Sorsha entered. "Are you alright?" she asked.

Crissy blinked and nodded. "I dropped a box in the closet."

Sorsha placed her hands on Crissy's shoulders. "I know you did not want to lose the cabinets. I had hoped they would pick them up and be gone before you returned from town. But the chance of finding your sister..." Tears rolled down her cheeks. "Sabine is more valuable than the cabinets."

Crissy's throat tightened. "Father built them."

"Perhaps someday you can get them back. Wouldn't you rather Sabine return home?"

"She ran away from us," Crissy said as she let tears flow.

Sorsha wrapped her arms around her and pulled her close. "I don't know why she would do that. We must ask one day, when she is home." Sorsha's voice cracked. She released Crissy and wiped her face. "I will see you at dinner."

Crissy breathed once Sorsha left the room and closed the door behind her. She pulled her hair into a braid. When she lifted the blanket from off the book, the image of a wolf in the margins captured her attention. She sat to read.

Chapter 3

Old bones. Sabine lifted her hand to the beam of light streaming through the freshly washed windowpane. Through the glow of her wrinkled flesh, she could see veins and tendons. With a sigh, she dropped her arm and turned to the front door. How long had it been since she pulled the bench from the kitchen to the wall, offering a place to sit and watch through the open door. She hobbled to the worn bit of furniture and flopped down with a heave of frustration. She leaned her head against the moss-colored wall and bit her lip. She could feel her heart pounding in her chest. Her eyes drifted closed. Tired. But tiredness did not feel right.

Sabine jumped to her feet. A haze filled the air. She turned and saw the old woman asleep on the bench. Silver white hair, braided, fell across her shoulder. Sabine reached for her own blonde braid. She rubbed her hands along the length as she stared at the old woman. Sallow cheeks, thin yet wrinkled. Her skin seemed stretched. She wore a simple gray dress with a neat apron. Sabine looked down. It was the same apron she wore. She wiped the palms of her hands on it. Her feet were bare, and the weathered boards of the porch, heated by the afternoon sun, warmed her feet as she stepped through the door of the house.

The front needed to be swept, but the pull of birds fluttering through the garden drew her instead. She skipped down the steps and twirled, arms outstretched.

A person flashed across her vision. She slowed to a stop and let her arms drift down. It had been so long since she had seen anyone but the old woman who slept all the time, she could only stare.

His clothing was rough and well-worn with patched elbows and faded knees. The shirt was no longer white. She could see a brown vest beneath the jacket. Hair covered his jaw and chin, yet it was trimmed. The skin of his face and hands appeared tanned. This was a man who lived out of doors, in God's open lands. Why was he here?

From the look on his face, he was as puzzled as she. His blue eyes glanced from her to the house, and back to her.

"I am dreaming." The rumble of his voice pleased her ears.

She looked at the house. It stood as it had as long as she could remember. The blue accents had faded a bit, but she couldn't climb that high to paint them fresh. If she had fresh paint with which to accomplish the task. The house held a mixture of age and charm, but nothing particularly dreamy about it. "It isn't that great a place."

"No. I must have fallen asleep waiting for Graham to return."

"Then you have joined my dream? I've not known that to happen before."

"I'm dreaming you."

"But I was here before you arrived. Came from inside the house. How could I have been thinking and doing if I am merely a member of your dream?"

He stepped closer. "I don't know. This is the first time I've dreamt like this." He poked a finger at her arm.

She slapped him away. This wasn't a dream. Or if it was, it was her dream.

He frowned. "What do you do, if you are more than a dream."

"I live here with an old woman."

"Your grandmother?"

She shrugged. "I'm not sure. She sleeps whenever I am awake. The poor dear works herself too hard. And you? What do you do?"

"I hunt." He pulled the crossbow from his shoulder. "Not for pleasure, mind you. I see that look of disgust."

Sabine allowed her lip to remain curled in disdain.

"Wild animals can become dangerous."

"Is that why you are here?"

"But I'm not, I'm asleep. The land is open, no forest in which to hide."

He stood close enough that she raised her head to talk with him. His blue eyes shimmered and lips twitched. He was years older, though she doubted he was old. The hand she'd hit felt real enough.

Something tugged at her back, like a hand grabbed the cloth of her dress and yanked her toward the door. She stumbled a bit. "Guess it's time to go."

"Wait, no." he tried to grab her, but she moved backward, her arms cartwheeling. She should have fallen over, but something held her upright.

The woods, him, everything faded.

Sabine opened her eyes, air rattled in her chest as she drew a deep breath. She leaned forward, facing the door. The sun still shone. The trees swayed in whatever breeze moved them from above. Birds sang. But there was no man. No young woman. She pushed herself to her feet and felt pain radiate through her knees. The view outside was beautiful, but her heart thrummed with terror the closer she came to the door. She must never leave.

Chapter 4

Patrick woke with a start. The image of the woman and strange dream lingered in his mind. Late afternoon sun streamed through the edges of closed shutters. The time had come to hunt.

He tugged his leather vest over his shirt and used the toggle to fix it tight. His fingers slid along a tear formed by the claw of a wolf. By the Creator's grace, the beast hadn't torn him worse.

Someone pounded on the door a moment before it flew open. "Birds have taken flight over the trees."

Patrick gazed past the man at the late afternoon. "The turning of the year causes many of them to swarm south."

"Or wolves are lurking. I've paid you to rid us of them. Send the foul beasts back to hell."

Patrick frowned. "They are no more of hell than you or I. So long as they haven't attacked a human, I will capture and take them beyond the settled lands."

"I paid you to kill."

Patrick tightened his fists. "You paid to rid them

from your farm." He motioned to the waning day. "Time wastes."

It wasn't that he refused to kill, but the creatures were majestic. It was only after they got a scent for human blood and flesh that there was no other recourse. The beasts attacking the farm went after pigs and chickens, no signs they traveled close to the cottage.

He swung his crossbow into place on his shoulder and slid a dagger into a holder on his thigh. A howl carried across the land as he sauntered into a field heavy with barley. He headed toward a thicket of trees at the top of a hill.

From the snarling he heard whipping around him, at least two creatures were trapped. The first trap held a young male with ears back and teeth snapping at the wooden cage. The animal fought. Its pelt was thick graying brown and well-formed muscles rippled as it tried to escape.

Patrick held his breath as he pulled a blanket from the crook of a branch. He removed the fleece and laid it on the trap, stepping back several feet before sucking breath into his body. The frenzy of the wolf continued for a moment, and then the scuffling quieted. Its snarls turned to yips. Then with a gurgle and a thud, there was silence.

He turned to the other trap several hundred feet away and repeated his actions. There were no other signs of wolves. Patrick frowned. acks were larger than two. He used ropes to pull the cages onto his wagon. The potion on the blankets would last long enough to get the beasts away from the farm and others in the community. He checked the other traps and freshened chicken carcasses used for bait. As he drove into the moonlight, thoughts of his strange dream mingled with the shadows.

Chapter 5

As the sun dipped behind the house, Crissy moved into the forest. In her hand she gripped a pouch holding Sabine's clothes, hairbrush, and a ratted long eared stuffed rabbit. She'd taken the things from her sister's bedroom. Two years, and they wanted it kept the same. She pushed memories of playing with Sabine as a baby, the way her blue eyes sparkled when Crissy swung her in circles. Their laughter across the yard. This was their fault, Mother and Oleg. Crissy just wanted to keep what was rightfully hers. What father had left for her. She swiped at tears on her cheeks. It wasn't fair that Sabine had to die, but what choice remained?

When it grew too dark, she opened her lantern. Her feet seemed to know the way, though her heart remained heavy with guilt and dread. Rustling among the brush let her know something drew close. Her breath tightened. Perhaps the wolves would kill her, and she could join her father. Shadows moved. A creature drew closer to her circle of light. It was smaller than she thought, thin, with silent paws. An intelligence gleamed from its yellow eyes. There were more. She could feel them around her. She clutched the package against her heart. It waited. Its direct gaze drew her in. It was beautiful. Awe dripped through the pain of what she needed to do. She tossed the pouch at its feet.

When they were gone, she followed. How could she not? But the snarls she heard weren't what she expected. Crissy doused the lantern, not wanting Sabine to see her from the ancient house. In the moonlight, Crissy saw wolves pacing along the edge of the clearing. Yet they could not step any closer. Their yips brought Sabine to a window. Crissy stepped behind a tree. The old woman gazed from within the house. Fearful. But the wolves could not draw any closer. Crissy closed her eyes. The spell on Sabine must be the stronger spell. Others would have to be sacrificed, strengthening the wolves until they could not be deterred.

Crissy gripped the lantern as she returned to the main path. She tripped on something, catching herself before she fell. The bag with Sabine's things lay in the dirt. She retrieved it and turned toward the village. She didn't have to go far when giggles sounded among the trees. She closed the lantern. Someone else had come.

Two lights showed a man and a woman in a passionate embrace. She recognized Jedison Torr. The sight of his bare back caused heat in her belly. He'd never kissed her like that. The opportunity seemed perfect. Neither one noticed when Crissy darted forward and stole his shirt. She raced back. It didn't take long for the wolf to find her. She tossed the shirt in its path. The desire to see what would happen next drew her to follow. Screams rent the melody of night in the forest. They were close enough to the village that someone would come. Crissy barely got a view of two beasts tearing into Jedison's chest. The girl just stood there screaming.

News of the attack blazed through the village the following day. Crissy smirked. It hadn't been an innocent walk through the woods in the moonlight. Sorsha refused to let Crissy leave the house. It wasn't until night had fallen when she was finally able to sneak away. She had the bag of Sabine's things. Once again, she dropped it for the wolf. Was it her imagination, or had the beast grown? The light from its eyes gleamed with evil intent. Had she done that to it? She followed, but the wolves could barely move into the clearing. Disappointment caused her shoulders to droop as she returned to her bedroom. She placed the bag of Sabine's things in her closet beneath a mound of clothes where it wasn't likely to be found by anyone else. She closed her eyes and breathed. More sacrifices would need to be made.

Chapter 6

G randmother, are you here?"

The muscles at the nape of Sabine's neck clenched. Why did she visit? Youth draped over the girl like a curse. She strangled her with it. The basket of food and goodies was appreciated, but the old had no use for youth.

She hobbled to the hall, resting her hand against the bench. The girl, supposedly her granddaughter, stood on the stairs. The young face brightened. Sabine wanted to slap the grin away. Her chest burned. What about the young woman caused such anguish?

"You look tired."

Sabine frowned. "I am old. You will know the sting of age as well."

"That is an awful thing to say Grandmother." The girl frowned. "You lived your life, is it not fair that I live mine as well?"

Had she lived a life? Sabine tried to recall. "I have no memory of my life. Not living it."

"Poor dear. It is a wretched fate, grandmother."

"Why are you here?"

The red cape the girl insisted on wearing

billowed as she raised her arm. "I bring goods. Cans to store for the winter."

"Bring it around to the kitchen, my arms are too weary for such a task."

But the young woman shook her head. "You will not step through the doorway, and neither will I." She bent and placed the basket on the ground. She pushed it through the door with her foot.

Sabine put both hands across her belly. It was too close to the outside. Much too close.

"Come, Grandmother, let me see you take the basket."

"Devil take you, girl."

"I am sorry, Sabine. For all of this. But you do not have much longer to wait."

Of what did she speak? The girl was daft. Sabine shook her head.

The young woman watched for a moment, and then skipped away, going through the trees until she could see her no longer. Instead, Sabine stared at the basket. She shuffled a few steps closer. The air heated and her head spun. Every time. The girl tormented her. Could it be for a purpose? She took another step closer. Tears stuck to the back of her throat. Fear. Why such anguish? What could be beyond the door that caused such a feeling?

Chapter 7

W hat do you hunt?"

Patrick turned and found himself facing the young woman. His pulse quickened. How was it possible?

"You cannot be real." He stroked her cheek.

Her eyes widened, and she pulled away. Her hand covered where he had touched her. She opened her mouth as if to speak but remained silent.

"You aren't real, are you?" Patrick stared at her.

"I don't know what I am. I walk in twilight."

"Are these woods safe in the night?"

"I had thought so, but wolves have been here."

"Wolves? How can you tell?"

She motioned him to follow. He allowed her to lead him through the side yard, circumventing a stone fence. When she stopped, she pointed at the ground. There were footsteps, at least two fully grown wolves tramped across the dampened earth. "They should not be this close to a settlement." He looked at the house. "Is the old woman ill?" That could draw them.

The girl shook her head. "She is well enough, sleeps often."

"Wolves can be dangerous. If they have tracked this close to your house, you would do well to remain inside. Or make your way to town until the pack moves on for winter."

"I do not think we can go to town."

"Is there one nearby?"

She tilted her head and looked at the forest. "Somewhere beyond. I think there is. Dover, perhaps? I lived there once, long ago."

"If you are real, then mayhap I can come to help."

"Help what?"

He waved, encompassing the clearing and the house. "This. You. The place that calls me in my dreams."

A moment later, she was gone. The trees were gone. He lay beneath a starry sky where gentle bare hills rolled to the horizon. Just a dream. And yet, as he stood, stretching his arms over his head, he wondered if such a place could exist. "Dover." The name sounded natural enough. Perhaps it was time to move on.

Chapter 8

Grandmother's basket is ready, Crissy." Sorsha used a linen towel to cover the prepared meal.

Crissy finished rubbing oil into the maple chest. Its surface gleamed. The rose-banded China packed inside was intended for her wedding and the house she would start with her husband. *But I intend to keep this place.* She looked around the formal living room. The walls had been papered in yellow with vertical lines of ivy. Two formal chairs flanked the bay window with a sofa set across from them.

She replaced the lace runner across the chest as Sorsha stepped into the arched opening.

"Will you take the basket to Grandmother? Your father has not yet returned."

Crissy looked at the floor. The tightly woven rug had twisted vines across it. "He's looking for her, isn't he?"

"He still hopes to find her."

"What about me? I'm here, I didn't run away." She glanced at Sorsha as she blinked moisture from her eyes. *Why should it matter, he wasn't her real father.*

"He loves you, Crissy. Believe me. He just can't let Sabine go."

"It's been two years."

"When you have children of your own, you will understand." She lifted the basket. "Will you take the meal to Grandmother?"

"Yes, Mother."

"Wear your red cape, there's a chill in the air. And stay on the path. Stories are going around about wolf packs."

"You tell me the same thing every trip." She grabbed the handle of the basket.

"Be back before nightfall. We'll have dinner at eight."

"Yes, Mother."

"Tell Grandmother hello. Ask if she has needs."

Crissy kissed Mother's cheek. "This is not my first visit. I will see you at dinner come eight o'clock."

It wasn't her first visit. She'd been taking the paths into the woods for two years, though Sorsha and Oleg would say it had been forever. The main street through town had been paved with square bricks. Crissy hopped over the white ones, swinging the basket forward and backward. She passed the houses built with thin gardens between them, crossed over Macie's fence, and made her way to the wooded path. Blue sky peeked through the branches until the trees became twisted together and twilight settled along the path. Sometime later, after a sharp curve, Grandmother's house came into view. Candles burned in the windows, causing Crissy's mouth to twist. *Never did like the dark, did you*?

With quiet feet, she snuck up the stairs and across the porch. The front door stood open. Inside looked cheery. Two chairs were set by the thick kitchen table. The counter was clear of debris. A fire whipped in the fireplace. Crissy smiled. A quaint little home for an old woman. Only Sabine wasn't really old.

"Grandmother? Are you home?" Crissy called out.

Something thumped, words she couldn't understand, and then the bent old woman leaning on her cane moved into view.

"There you are," Crissy waved. "Thought maybe you went into town."

"Don't tease, little girl." Sabine narrowed her rheumy eyes. "You know I'll not step over that threshold. An evil world it is out there. Here I will stay, thank you very much."

"I'm not little anymore, Grandmother. I'm twenty now." Crissy swirled. "Don't I look grown up?"

"You look like trouble." Sabine inched closer. She breathed deeply and rubbed her back.

"Feeling old today?"

"As will you. Someday." She stared at something beyond Crissy's shoulder. "The world looks the same. I am the only one who aged."

"You enjoyed long life."

"Have I? I dream of my youth, at times chasing after you. I dream, and yet I remember nothing." She leaned against the door jam. "Not growing up. No beau. Marriage? Children? You are my granddaughter, there must be children. Why have I no memory of them?"

"Perhaps it is easier that way." She lifted the basket. "Here is food."

Sabine raised her skinny arm and reached for the handle. Her hand passed over the threshold of the door. Crissy watched the wrinkled flesh smooth, dark spots fading to creamy skin. She pushed the basket through the doorway and saw the hand turn old once more. Sabine staggered back with it.

"It's heavy today."

"Mother was expecting guests. There's chicken pie, apples from the orchard, and cobbler. I think she cut fall vegetables as well. Winter's coming, you'll have canned goods."

"Your mother is a good woman. Must be busy, never visits."

"I like coming, Grandmother. It is good to see you."

"Best run along. Night will be setting shortly. Beware of wolves. I've seen them strolling through the woods. Not safe, not for anyone."

"Don't worry, Grandmother," Crissy smirked, "they can't get in your home. Not yet anyhow." The old woman didn't hear the last few words. Crissy turned toward home but paused to peek at the side of the house. There were fresh prints in the dirt. The wolves came close. Her chest pounded. More sacrifices needed to be made. A shiver crossed her skin as she pondered who would be worth achieving her goals.

Chapter 9

The town existed. Patrick noticed the trees beyond. Somewhere in the woods could be a young woman living with her grandmother. Or his mind had taken a wrong turn.

People clustered in the street. The tones of their voices were hushed, and their shoulders seemed tight.

"Morning," he tipped his hat to an older gentleman crossing the road.

The man looked him up and down with a grunt. "There's no good in this morning."

Patrick was puzzled at the cold greeting. "I seek a room for hire."

The man pointed to a two-story structure further into town. "Gunthers has plenty of space. No one will want to remain after news spreads."

"News? Something bad has happened?"

"That it has." He tugged on his beard. "Never heard the like. An entire family gone. Murdered."

"Murdered?" Patrick folded his arms to ward off a chill. "Does a madman live here?"

"Not human. A pack of wolves turned ravenous. We've seen 'em, they been here a while. But this?

Never imagined this sort of behavior."

"Wolves? How can you be sure?"

"It was them animals, right enough. Acting more like a devil than God's creatures."

"Walk with me to Gunthers. I may be able to help."

~

The next day, Crissy sat across the dining table from Oleg. Not quite tall, having a plump body, the man would have been considered jovial if circumstances hadn't taken his true daughter from him. In two years, he hadn't been able to forget, so though he smiled, sadness lingered in his eyes. His lips didn't rise quite as high as they might have.

"You look tired, Father." Though not hers by birth, he'd asked her to call him that, preferring Sabine to think of them as a real family.

He took a sip from the wine goblet. "Home is a good place to be. I am thankful to return to you."

People could easily be taken, death's touch cared little for young or old. But this house, the possessions within, these were the things for which she yearned. Things that belonged to her because they had been her father's. Some might try to take them from her, but they would not succeed. The book she had found reassured her.

"… Beckett homestead appears to be wolves."

Crissy's attention perked. She looked up from her soup bowl.

"The family was murdered, their bodies ripped…"

"Oleg," Sorsha admonished him with a glare.

But Crissy wanted more details. "The Beckett

family? Who was killed?"

"The dinner table is not the place for such conversation." Sorsha rebuked them both.

"We will talk later this evening. The Mayor and the Kaughmans will join us."

"Whatever for?" Crissy couldn't remember a time when guests were brought in that late.

"Wolves have tasted blood. They will not stop until they are killed. We need to hire hunters."

Sorsha looked pale, but she remained calm. "Then this conversation may wait until our guests have arrived."

Alexander Fairmoore and Gunter Erhardt arrived first, followed by Eibella and Dietrich Kaughman. A stranger joined them, a man of indiscriminate height. Though his dark hair had been slicked and tied back and his beard trimmed, he reeked of wild. His clothes were pleasant enough, probably borrowed from Mayor Fairmoore, Crissy thought. She felt his eyes on her as she poured tea and prepared a tiny dish with jelly-printed cookies dusted with sugar. She narrowed her eyes at him, but he didn't even have the gall to appear embarrassed to be caught watching.

"Your guest?" Oleg shook hands with the mayor.

Mayor Fairmoore smiled broadly; his round cheeks puffed out. "An answer to prayer, you will see. Our Lord God prepares his response nary the words have left our lips."

"What?" Oleg looked at the man.

"Word of the packs has spread," the man's voice grated, "though I did not hear of tragedy until arriving in town this afternoon." He slapped the mayor's shoulder, as men were prone to do. "Met Fairmoore at the Inn. The public rooms were in an uproar."

"Terrible business." Dietrich shook his head.

"The family was slaughtered." Mayor Fairmoore looked at her.

Crissy gulped.

"Unpleasant business for a girl, are you sure you should be here?" The stranger asked.

Why should he care for her delicacy? Crissy handed a plate to the mayor and squared her shoulders. "More right than you to be here."

"Lass, I mean you no disrespect—"

"They are known to me. It is unpleasant to hear what has become of them, and I sorrow for the children. But I am of age, I will know what has happened and what is planned to deal with the problem."

"Crissy speaks truth." Oleg sighed. "Terrible things we must all face. What is your name, stranger, seeing you speak freely in my home?"

"I beg your pardon, sir." He offered a nod. "Patrick Slattery."

"You have the sound of the island in your speech."

"Aye, that is true, sir. The wilds of Iveragh. I'm a hunter. You are bound to get more of us as news of the attack spreads."

"We'll be grateful for your service, Mr. Slattery."

"Wolf is as I'm known."

Of course, he would be, Crissy thought with a

frown.

Later that evening, moonlight splashed through the bedroom window. Crissy did not require a lantern to lace her boots, but she lit it and wrapped the silver case around the glass to block the light. With her room located at the back of the house, she easily slid over the windowsill and landed on the soft layer of mulch laid to winter the garden. Round footstones marked the path through the garden. The gate creaked as she pushed it open. The light of the full moon could not penetrate the woods. Crissy knelt beside a fallen log and lifted the lantern glaze, pulling away the silver lining. A soft glow encased her, and she could see the first pair of twisted tree trunks leading into the forest. She stepped around them. The rough track swept down a shallow ravine. She held the lantern aloft and pulled herself up to the far side. She took a few more steps through the underbrush and found one of the paths leading through the forest.

Crissy passed the trail she took to Sabine, skirting the heart of the woods for the western edge. Something moved to her left. Beyond the edge of light, a shadow followed her, matching step for step. More than one. She could hear their feet pattering across the uneven ground. She stopped, placed the lantern on the ground, and wrapped the silver lining around the glass. Darkness descended around her; her eyes could not yet decipher any of the ambient shine pouring down from the stars. She could hear movement, smell the musky pelts of wolves.

She stretched her hand out, and for a moment

nothing happened. Then something nuzzled her hand. Amazing creatures. Lean, hard bodies were covered with thick, soft fur. Predators, cunning and deadly, yet they cared for their young, watched over them.

"You must be swift, my dears. Strengthen yourselves with human blood until you can break the threshold. Beware, hunters are come."

Beneath her hand, the body of the wolf tightened, and she felt its growl of understanding. She drew a small shirt from her pocket. Crissy gripped the shoulders and flapped it open and then laid it on the ground. She didn't think about the child, nor his brothers and sisters. She thought of Sabine. Her father had searched long for his daughter, imagine his shock at finding her ravished body deep in the woods. The wolves would break the spell surrounding the house and destroy Grandmother.

"What big eyes you have," Crissy imagined the wrinkled, rheumy orbs opening in fright.

"What big ears you have." Snarling and growling would be the last sounds she heard.

"And what big teeth you have." Screams would not linger. The wolves tore into the neck of their victims first, allowing blood loss to weaken their prey to the point of surrender.

Poor Sabine, such an end after two years of enchantment. Crissy's heart ached for a moment. But Sabine wasn't her blood. The new man, claiming to be her father, intended Sabine to inherit another man's toil. Her father had provided wealth and riches, not Sabine's. He had merely taken what belonged to another. Hatred burned, wrapped up in sorrow and anger. Sabine was a pawn. Look at the way he searched for her, and what he had sold to pay for it.

Crissy shook herself, drawing her mind to the woods and the surrounding night. Wolves had dispersed. She crumpled the blue shirt and shoved it into her pocket. Cherga Genbach filled the lines at the back of their garden with clothes. Seven sons and a girl. Prey, helpless against the power of the wolves. With the brief scent given to them, they would track to the family farm. Crissy slowed her steps, imagining. The pack would use the shadows, making their way around the house, searching for an opening, a weakness. A window left un-shuttered; a doorway cracked open to allow air to circulate. Silent and swift, they would move into the house, to the rooms where human warmth drew them. Take out the youngest first, the smallest, and then work their way to the adults, Cherga and her chunky husband. The smell of blood would soak into the wood, mixed with the pungent odor of wolf. Torn flesh, feast. Power would flow through them. How many more would need to be sacrificed before the spell surrounding Sabine could be broken?

Crissy quickened her pace. Time was essential. Another attack would draw more hunters. She uncovered the lantern and traced her steps toward home. A different noise captured her attention. Leaves crunching underfoot. Someone else moved nearby. Too close to her to put out the light, they would have seen her. She raised the lantern. "Show yourself."

"Not what I expected to find in the woods tonight."

Him. Wolf. She held her snarl inside. His hands should be dripping in wolf blood. How many of the majestic creatures had been slaughtered by them?

"I fear for my grandmother. I meant to stay the night with her, but I could not find her path. The darkness has twisted my way."

He moved closer. With his dark clothes, he hid well among the shadows. But where were his weapons?

He spoke, an edge of distrust in his tone. "You are alone in the dark? Perfect bait for the pack."

"I did not intend…"

"Yet here you are, folly of a young mind."

"Be my guide home. Surely the hunter can prevent himself from becoming prey?"

He laughed, a dry humorless noise. "I'm sure you could teach me a thing about predators and prey, Miss Bostich. What will tomorrow reveal to us?"

"I do not take your meaning, sir. I tire. Hunt your beasts." She peered at his empty hands. "Though I know not what you will do against them without arrow or sword."

"In due course. Their unusual behavior draws me."

"As you please. I mean to follow the trail home."

He backed away and disappeared into the night. Crissy didn't bother looking for him, she continued home. Shivers coursed her back as she imagined his eyes following her.

~

Wolf watched as Miss Bostich wound her way along the path leading out of the woods. Her dark hair and fair skin should have piqued his interest, but the lovely young woman caused his heart to clench. An aura of darkness surrounded her.

Somewhere ahead, snarls and a yelp drew his attention. More snarls and then a piercing cry sounded. After that, it was silent. Minutes passed before the usual sounds of night rose in volume. It did not take much longer to find something. A wolf lay on the path.

The animal's coat was a molten mix of gray, white, and black. Laying on its side, breath shallow and fast, it looked more to be pitied than feared. He slowed his steps, rustling leaves beneath his feet. The wolf shook its head but appeared unable to rise.

A mortal wound cut into its side. Wolf searched the nearby trees, but no other animals hid. Why had they not finished it off? The creature had sad eyes. Pained eyes. Where were the signs of rabid behavior? He touched her coat, well away from the wound. She whimpered.

"Are you not one of the wolf pack?" But this was no evil beast. He pulled his knife. Death would be upon her soon enough, but he could lessen the length of anguish to be endured.

After the deed had been accomplished, he resumed tracking the others.

Chapter 10

Crissy sat at the upper story window in the nook between bedrooms. A group of villagers lingered outside the General Store. She couldn't hear their whispered words, but frequent glances toward the woods suggested their topic of conversation revolved around the wolves. Mrs. Rhinebach, matron of the store, covered her mouth.

Crissy straightened as Wolf walked to the group. Being found by him during the night did not please. He was a tracker. Care must be taken until he could be dealt with. How could she obtain an article of his clothing? Beside him, Mayor Fairmoore pulled a watch from his vest. Others nodded. Reluctance to leave her solitude pulled at her, yet a plot was being concocted. She placed a ribbon in the book that had sat idle in her lap and headed for the stairs.

Wolf latched on to her almost as soon as she crossed the street. "You found your way home?"

She twirled to face him, putting a fake smile on her face. "Kind of you to inquire. I did not realize you were familiar with the Rhinebach's."

"My popularity grows. Another family has been butchered."

She nodded. "I heard. Horrifying, to think I was in the region as well."

"Your Grandmother should come to town if you fear her safety."

"She will not leave her home. I have never known her to step through the doorway."

"Will you take me to meet her? Perhaps I may convince her of the necessity."

Did he doubt there was a grandmother? Crissy tilted her head. "You may have charm, sir, but you have yet to convince me you are an honorable man. You, too, were in those woods last evening. Did you not cross paths with the wolves?"

"Only with you. I was distracted."

"Perhaps tonight you will be more successful. What is the plan? I saw several of the men confer with Mayor Fairmoore."

"We will meet at Luxley Hall this afternoon. Your father will be one of the men joining us."

"May I accompany him?"

"Plenty of curious ears." Wolf smiled, yet his eyes remained wary. "The ladies plan to prepare a meal, though I suspect more effort will go toward listening than cooking."

Females, especially those living in the village, were nosy to a fault. "I will see you this afternoon. What time did you say?"

"Two-of-the-clock."

They parted ways. Luxley Hall marked the center of town. The green square to the front was often used for festivals and many windows opened to it. Its large main room easily held everyone in the town. It was a grand building meant to impress both locals and strangers. Crissy headed away from it. Her father's house was infinitely better.

As the autumn sun lowered that afternoon, Oleg chose to take the carriage, allowing Sorsha and Crissy to ride in comfort, as well as to make room for a pair of black bird pies freshly baked. The main room of the hall was full when they arrived, people from the village and surrounding lands mulling in groups of various sizes. Crissy wandered aimlessly, staring at the floor as murmurings rose around her. Horror at the death of children. Lives lost. Torn asunder. The attack had been brutal. She shuddered thinking about it. The pack had gained strength.

Someone would have to be next. Plenty of farms surrounded the main village. How to choose a worthy sacrifice?

Wolf's voice carried across the crowd. Crissy cringed, though she could not hear what he said. How many wolf pelts had he carved from carcasses? Death stalked his steps. But a single victim would not be enough. Someday soon, he and her sister could feel the bite of fangs, the tear of claws. He was more deserving than Sabine. Another young life that would be cut short, but sister dearest stood between Crissy and security. It wasn't to be borne. She stood at a window and stared at the lawn that had turned brown by the cooling days.

"Doesn't seem fitting for the sun to shine on such a bleak afternoon." Wolf made his way to her side.

Crissy sighed. "Death is a natural part of our life

here."

He shook his head in disagreement. "Wolves do not attack in this manner. Within walls? Dragging children from their beds?"

Crissy narrowed her eyes. *What implication did he wish to impart*? "You think something other than wolves did this? Some dark blight that hunts the night? Has your mind been turned by Gothic tales?"

"There is no doubt the animals killed the family. But it is not their instinct to behave in such a way."

"Dark dealings." Mayor Fairmoore joined them. "To live through such times is difficult to fathom."

His vest stretched across a wide belly. The dark hair at his temples had become peppered with gray. Crissy glanced beyond, where his wife, Eloise, stood with a brood of friends. Their voices supported the general hum throughout the room.

"It is a tragedy, sir." Crissy offered a weak smile. He was a good mayor, lived in town but his house had been built on the hill, far enough apart to give the appearance of separation. Elevation. The house included children. A grandmother. Maids and other servants. A massive household, many more victims than the Genbach's.

"We will meet at the smithy at dusk." Wolf was shaking hands.

Crissy returned her attention to the conversation that had been drifting around her. "Meet?" Wolf's dark eyes made her want to back away. He didn't trust her.

"It is past time to hunt these beasts." The mayor tucked his hands in his pockets. "At least thirty men will join us. We will take the woods tonight.

Carcasses will foul the town center come morning. Wolf carcasses, not human."

Her smile came easily. Yes, into the woods. Would they think about protecting the streets and houses they left behind? The mayor would enter the front cubicle of his house and find bloody prints across the marble. No. His sacrifice would be needed as well. It needed to be all of them.

"Not a night to wander to Grandmother's house," Wolf admonished.

"Grandmother?" Mayor Fairmoore looked from one to the other, "Didn't she have an ancient looking place deep in the woods? Near the broken oak. I would think her long dead."

"Old, certainly, but not dead." Crissy reassured him. "Refuses to step from her home. Insane as a lark on dewberries, but she's harmless."

"Let us hope she does not draw the attention of the pack." Wolf stared at her. He couldn't know what she planned, but he suspected something.

"They seem intent on larger prey. Well, more numerous, anyway."

"Why is that do you suppose?"

She shrugged. Vile man. Someday he would know the truth. It would be her pleasure to enlighten him.

An hour later, Crissy knelt beside her bed and pulled the handle on the shallow trunk stored beneath the straps of the bed frame. She drew the locket from her neck and lifted the key from its compartment. A twist of metal, the click of a lock opening, and she raised the lid.

Daylight streaming through the window

revealed the musty leather-bound book. The secure chest proved a much better hiding spot than a shelf in the closet. Her fingers trailed over the cover. Ah, the power. Her flesh crawled with goose bumps, but she could no more turn from it than she could cut off her arm. She lifted the book from the chest. She cleared her mind and focused on the challenge. Get into Mayor Fairmoore's house unseen. This family hung no laundry in the garden. The task would be harder, more dangerous. But the reward—time to finish what was started four years ago. The villagers would hunt the wolves to the ground and destroy them. She needed the wolves to accomplish their ultimate purpose before that happened. Kill Sabine. Secure Christine's inheritance.

~

Wolf joined a group of men at a tall round table. Talk lingered on the woods, the wolves hiding among the trees. "What of places within the woods? Have houses been built? Carpenters, or loggers perhaps? Woodsmen?"

"Crissy Bostich heads into the woods frequently." A burly gray-haired man nodded, taking a swig of beer. "We all recognize that red cloak she wears. Caries a basket full of goodies, she's taking it to someone."

His slim cousin pointed around the table with the end of his pipe. "That old grandmother of theirs."

"An old woman?" Wolf leaned closer. "She lives in a Victorian house?"

"Not sure what kind of house it be. Never seen it." The man chewed on the pipe for a moment, then pointed it at him once more. "Nothing good in those trees."

"Hogwash. You've naught but a suspicious mind." The old man with a scar above his right eye turned to Wolf. "Think I saw it as a lad. Not sure how much could be left."

"Is there a map?"

He cackled. "A map?" He tapped his head with his finger. "This here's me map. I worked in those woods as a young man. The paths haven't changed much since then, I warrant."

"I have paper at my quarters. Could you show me the paths to take?" He tried not to let excitement buzz, but his fingers tingled. His feet longed to go.

Chapter 11

C rissy wrapped the red cloak around herself, securing it with a clasp around her neck. She drew the hood over her head. Speaking words from the book, she watched color seep away. A glance in the mirror revealed merely a shadow. Excitement flowed through her veins.

For late afternoon, the streets were empty. Fear kept people indoors, as though wood and metal could stop the beasts breaking through. They would have what they wanted. What she wanted.

Crissy walked to the tree-shaded edge of the street. A shadow moving in the open sunlight would draw unwanted attention. The glimmer would not stand up to careful watch. The lane turned, curving around the hill. The mayor's driveway, lined with oaks, took a more direct route to the top. She had walked it before, many times in fact. For parties. Dances. Midsummers Eve and Boxing Day. Two of the children were her age, unmarried yet. The others were younger. Sadness tugged at her heart, and yet, to offer such a sacrifice… they were lovely. Innocent.

The house on the hill appeared grand with its

marble columns and wide yard. She skirted the front, knowing the kitchen door was most likely to be open and unwatched at this time.

There it was. The simple brown door and shadowy beyond. The smell of pies wafted through the air.

Crissy paused at the window just to be certain. Though trees and sky reflected in the glass, there was none of her. Pleasure rushed through her.

Eager to accomplish the task, she stepped into the house. The back stairs led to the maids' room with its short hallway, then the nanny's quarters. Nothing moved in the back of the house. Crissy pressed her ear against the wood of the nanny's door. Silence. She eased the door slightly open and peaked through. Her breath caught in her throat and her heart pounded. The nanny sat in the rocker by the window. Crissy froze, watched, expected movement, chaos. But all she heard was a rumbling noise. The nanny snored.

She pushed the door open enough to slip through. Across the room, an open doorway led into the children's wing. It took little effort to cross the first bedroom, darting glances at the middle-aged woman cast across a chair with her jaw slacked open. The youngest pair of Fairmoore children were sleeping in their beds. One had discarded his shirt on the floor. Crissy picked it up and placed it in her pocket. She wanted more. Something belonging to the mayor.

She snuck through the room to the main hallway. It took two more doors before she found a large poster bed. The dainty nightgown laid across the spread would belong to Eloise Fairmoore. The delicate silk felt cool to the touch. Crissy twisted it into a ball and shoved it into the pocket as well. A tie lay discarded on a bureau. She added it to the growing collection.

Returning to the hallway, she heard footsteps on the stairs. Voices. She hurried to the children's wing of rooms, but a small dog trailed her.

"Cesar." Someone called for it.

The rascal had escaped its mistress to sniff at the edge of her cloak. Crissy paused at the door. Though the spell protected her from sight, opening and closing doors would be noticed. She kicked at the mutt with her booted foot. Rather than startling it away, the action seemed to entice it to play. With a yap, it jumped, bent the front two legs, and then pounced. Crissy swept her cape from its sharp little teeth, trying to push the dog further away without harm.

She rushed into the room, managed to close the door without letting the dog through. It scratched at the door, barking its displeasure. The boy in the first bed woke, sitting up and rubbing his eyes.

Crissy held her breath. Voices from the other side of the door yelled for the dog to cease its antics. Her heart stuck in her throat.

"What have you done, Jasper?" the older woman stepped through the other door. Crissy skirted them. The room was dim, shutters pulled to block the afternoon light probably to encourage sleep. Neither the boy nor his nanny seemed to notice her there. The woman moved to the boy's side as the hall door burst open. Crissy made it into the nanny's room before the dog could catch her. She continued on, retracing her steps. The voices faded as she made her way down the narrow stairs. Good thing no one rushed up from the kitchens.

But the lower rooms remained undisturbed by the commotion upstairs. She burst outside, picking up her skirts and running across the manicured garden to the protection of the line of trees. She gasped for breath, momentarily lightheaded. She threw the hood from her head as she leaned against the tree trunk. A glance to the side showed the house remained at peace.

She closed her eyes for a moment, drinking in the feel of victory. A cool breeze caressed her cheek. When she opened her eyes once more, she looked to the right, down the hillside toward town. Wolf walked a path a way off. Perhaps something else could be won this day as well. She covered her head and took to the shadows, following him into the woods.

He was trying to find Grandmother's house. Crissy watched him turn the paper in his hand upside down, look from the drawing to the turn in the path, then back at the drawing. He turned the map sideways. With a frustrated grunt, he crumpled the paper in his hand and shoved it into his pocket. Was it suspicion that drove him? Concern for an elderly woman alone in the woods? Did he fear the big bad wolves would get her? Crissy hoped so. Fervently. He pulled something from the satchel hanging at his side.

Wolf turned aside, but Crissy continued along the smaller path. Though it was still afternoon, twilight hovered among the trees. She left the trail at the broken tree. A bolt of lightning, many years before, had breached the thick trunk of an oak. One side had fallen against another tree while the other side remained fixed in the ground, though the tree itself had long since died. Skirting the standing trunk, she found the indent leading to the culvert. She crouched and waited. Wind whipped the tops of the trees, and she could hear the rustle of leaves and branches dancing in the canopy. No birds chirped. No insects buzzed. The forest remained hushed with the feel of magic.

A wolf brushed against her. Crissy drew the articles of clothing from the inside of her cloak and laid them across a litter of leaves. A pup pounced on the boy's shirt, tiny teeth digging into the fabric with a growl. Crissy backed away. Others joined the youngster, muzzles digging through the articles. Two wolves snapped at each other, tearing the nightgown.

"Stay clear of the deep woods tonight. Men will be hunting you." Nothing reacted to her words, yet she knew she'd been heard. Tonight, blood would run in the town. Tomorrow would be Sabine's turn. She returned to Luxley Hall.

Chapter 12

Men who seemed brave in the protection of the day, drooped with the setting sun. The moon had yet to rise, so only stars were present to guide their way. They brought a variety of weapons with them: pitchforks, axes with sharp blades, a pike, and some brandished swords that had been dug out from the storehouses. These were their weapons against the beasts. Did they think metal would protect them? Could they be quick enough to avoid the natural tone of swiftness and cunning imparted to the wolves? Crissy hid her grin. It mattered not. The wolves were closer than the villagers realized. Men would travel the paths among the trees in darkness, quaking in their shoes, and all the while the attack would occur on the hill. She turned to look at the house fading from sight. How soon before the pitter of paws on the steps? Across the marble floor? Silent up the back stairs. Would the children scream? The little boy and girl? What of the older ones? Would they try to throw something? Protect themselves? Or offer themselves as the intended sacrifice should? She sighed. It would have to wait till morning to know.

"Crissy, Father wants you home. This is not a night to visit with friends."

She turned to Sorsha. "The hall will be safe enough. Marlee and Idabell are here. Most everyone. We should wait for them to return. "

Sorsha looked at the main building with gas lights already lit. The sign moved in an easy breeze. Though the light illuminated much of the street where they remained, the men stalking toward the dark forest disappeared into the night.

"They shouldn't go." Sorsha moaned, rubbing her forehead. "How long can these animals last? Better to hide here and wait for winter's sting."

Crissy laid her arm across her shoulders and offered a hug. "We may hope they go unnoticed. Besides, they are greater in number."

"The Gerbach's numbered eleven. Slaughtered. How is it none escaped?"

"We are left to worry and pray. We should join the others, among friends. We will learn of their fate together."

Her mother searched her face, touched her cheek. "When did you grow, my daughter? How did age creep upon you without my notice?"

"There were other things occupying your thoughts. Come." Crissy took her mother's hand and pulled her across the room.

Eloise and her eldest daughter, Mary, stood at a long table. Crissy paused. She hadn't thought about that possibility. She would need to find a way to send them home on an errand soon.

"It's horrifying." Idabell grabbed her arm and pulled her from Sorsha. "We rode to the Vinci's and tried to convince them to join us in town. You remember Heinrich? He's asked me to stand with him during the Christmas ball. What will I do if he's murdered? The devil curse those foul beasts."

"Dear." Crissy patted her hand. "You are fraught over nothing. Attacks have been to the north. And what's this, standing up with Heinrich? Did he not dip your braids in the ink well when we sat in the schoolhouse together?"

Idabell blushed and lowered her head. "He always was attracted to my golden hair." She sighed, her eyes taking a distant glaze. "I watched him this summer, out in the field. The way his shirt stuck to his muscles…"

Crissy laughed. "Enough. You will have me needing a fan. Romance for you. A lovely thought."

"And what of you? Any members of our noble town capturing your fancy?" Idabelle glanced around. "All the men have taken to the woods, but surely someone has your attention. Or do you prefer the stranger?"

"Stranger?" Who…no. her brows furrowed. "You cannot mean the hunter? He is an old man."

"He is not old. Marlee thinks him quite handsome."

She crinkled her nose. "His hands are drenched with the innocent blood of animals. He desires valor and renown."

"He is handsome, intelligent, and determined. I thought you would admire such qualities." Idabelle shook her head. "If not, we will find another who will suit you. Perhaps you should travel to London."

"I am pleased to remain here." Crissy pointed

across the room. "I see Mrs. Fairmoore. I wonder if she has news."

The two girls crossed the hall. Candles burned against the walls, on the rough-hewn wood tables, and along the bar.

Mrs. Fairmoore twisted her hands. "The moon is just now rising. How will they find their way home? They must not remain in the woods for hours. The wolves will hunt them down."

"We've enough lights here to help them find their way."

Possibly, but Crissy could think of a better place. "What about your home? Light could be seen across the valley. You should have the windows lit."

Mrs. Fairmoore nodded. "Excellent idea, young lady. We'll remove the curtains, just to be safe. Mary, let us go home. We can set out the candlesticks we use at Christmastime."

"I will help," Sorsha offered, but Crissy grabbed her arm.

"You should stay. If there are any wounded when they return, they will have need of you."

Mrs. Fairmoore grasped Sorsha's hand. "Your daughter is right." She pressed her cheek against Sorsha's in a sign of farewell. "We must hurry. I don't want them out there longer than they need to be. Oh, this night feels foul."

Crissy breathed a sigh of relief as Mrs. Fairmoore and her daughter exited the hall. She took Sorsha's hand. "You should go home and rest. If they have need of you later, you will be ready."

She agreed. The large group of women began to

disperse. They walked the quiet streets like ghosts. Crissy watched as the women turned by twos and threes into alleys and cross streets. She and Sorsha followed the curve to their house.

"I will sleep on the sofa." Sorsha declared, heading for the front room.

"Your bed will be of more comfort. Remain dressed, that you can easily rise if the need occurs."

"Very well." She gave in with a tired sigh. "But fetch Henley. She must wait with me."

With Sorsha settled, Crissy slipped through the side door as she pulled her red cloak about her. The moon had risen higher, and curiosity burned. To be so close... but she would have to remain unseen. She slipped into the shadows and made her way to the bottom of the Fairmoore's hill. The line of oaks rose before her. Remaining on the side facing away from the house, she moved from the first tree to the next and the one after that. The night had gone completely still. She moved closer yet and was rewarded with the sound of a strangled cry. High pitched. Could it be Mary? Short lived. A guttural snarl whispered through the cold autumn night. Moonlight shone strong, but there was naught to see. Her heart pounded in her chest. They were there, she could feel them, but there was no sound. The wolves must have arrived before Eloise and Mary returned, for the lights in the windows had yet to be lit. Perhaps the mayor would do it, reverence to the sacrifice that had been made.

Crissy withdrew to her home, content in the workings of the night.

Chapter 13

A re you lost? No one ever comes this way."
Sabine crouched beside a blackberry bush.
Her fingers were stained with purple. The
woman paled, and Sabine jumped to her feet. "Are
you well? Should I fetch water?"

"What has happened?" The stranger looked at
the house, then returned her attention to Sabine.

"Naught that I am aware. Is there ill news from
town?"

The pale woman clenched her throat. "Have you
been to town?"

"Me? Gracious, no. My place is here. I'll not
leave her."

"Her? The old woman? Grandmother?"

Sabine frowned. How did this strange woman
know grandmother?

"I don't understand how this could be." She
took a step closer.

Sabine didn't like the way the strange woman's
eyes flickered. "Why are you here?"

She lifted the basket. "I bring food from Mother
and Father. Do you know them?"

Sabine backed away. "Why should I know your

parents? We have never met."

The stranger giggled and covered her mouth with her hand. She took a deep breath. "No, we haven't. Have we?"

Sabine watched as the other girl rushed into the woods. Odd. The man had been... friendlier? No, engaging. Handsome. But he hadn't been back in days. With a sigh, she returned to the house. The sound of a wolf's howl had her twisting to face the woods. Late autumn wind brushed against her, causing her skin to tingle.

~

Crissy jerked from sleep, shaking in her bed. A dream. Only a dream. An anxious chuckle tugged at her throat.

"Daughter, awake, we must flee." Sorsha burst into the room, causing the door to slam against the wall.

Crissy screamed. Sorsha paid no notice. She held on to the doorpost, her hand pressed against her mouth and tears streamed down her cheeks.

Crissy stared at her with wide eyes. "What?" She glanced at the window. Dawn barely touched the eastern sky.

"The wolves have attacked in town. We are not safe, not in this place. We will go to my sisters, across the river closer to London."

"Leave? Attack? What attack?" She sat up, the cloud of sleep not yet lifted from her mind. Sabine, she had been talking with Sabine.

"Mayor Fairmoore's family, the help, everyone. All of his children. And Eloise... we spoke with her last night." Mother's eyes looked huge. "We sent her home with Mary. They might have been spared had we not intervened."

"You know nothing of the sort." Crissy rubbed her cheeks. "The wolves attacked them inside their house?"

"The house on the hill. If the mayor is not safe, what about us? We will all be slaughtered, eaten by the devil's creatures."

"You make yourself overwrought, calm down." She crossed the room and took hold of her hands. "It must have been the lights in the windows. They drew the animals to them. The hunters in the woods sent the pack into the village."

Sorsha shook her head. "This place is cursed, there is no hope here. We must leave."

"What does Oleg say?" There was no way she was leaving. Sabine would finally meet her fate.

"He is with the mayor. You have never seen a man more changed."

Crissy could imagine the plump friendly demeanor would melt away. "We should go to the house."

"Absolutely not. Your father forbids. The sight…" She shook her head. "It is vile. The men could not walk the hallway without emptying their stomachs. No. You are to pack. We will leave before the noon hour."

She flopped back to the bed, arms crossed. Fear drove Sorsha, there would be no argument. Better to agree and take plans into her own hands. She closed her eyes, breathed deeply, then glanced at Sorsha without raising her head. "Fine. Allow me to pack in peace. I will alert our maid when my traveling box is prepared."

Sorsha gave a worried look through the glazed window. "Keep the shutters drawn. Our doom is near."

Sorsha was terrified. Crissy could see it in the paleness of her skin, deep circles beneath her eyes. The shivers along her arms. She wanted to draw her close. Reassure her their danger was nil. The urge to confess caused her own flesh to quiver, and her stomach turned. But Sorsha walked from the room, locked in her own torment, unaware. Crissy drew a shawl around her shoulders, but her hands continued to shake. What was this? This feeling of being torn? She had come too far, much too far. Blood taken. And more blood to be spilled. Sabine. And Wolf. She closed her eyes. Their deaths would release her from this ravening madness. She could forget, return to the age where innocence played among the trees. A sob cut her throat and she wiped tears from her cheeks.

She crossed to the wardrobe. She drew out the lower drawer and pulled at the board. In the tiny space beneath lay a red bag. She tugged it loose and held it against her belly. Her sister's things. Though her body trembled, she replaced the board and the drawer. The red cape floated around her as she adjusted the hook, not bothering to change from her night clothes. She shimmied the window and crawled from her room.

She had crossed the edge of the trees into the woods before she realized her feet were bare. Didn't matter. There was no going back. Crissy ran along the path. The air hummed with energy. Storms would rage across the valley ere night fell. An autumn storm that could end in snow. She made her way to the ravine where the wolves hid. Her heart pounded as her mind warred. Too late, much too late. It echoed in her head, even as she wondered at the new-found murmur to spare her sister. She couldn't love her. Couldn't care. Sabine had spent two years locked in enchantment. With a cry of frustration, she threw the bag. Everything stilled. She had done it. There was no going back. She had given Sabine to the wolves. She turned away.

Chapter 14

Crissy followed a different path to the village. Unlike the mad rush in, she walked calmly. Her mind cleared. No emotion raged within her. She felt… nothing. Victory was at hand and yet she felt empty. Void. It mattered not. Victory would be her comfort. A slight wind moved the air once she cleared the protection of the trees. Her nose wrinkled at the bitter smell. It smelled as though wood burned. Early for a fire, but the sting of cool could make it necessary. Another waft of smoke passed her. Wood burning, she was certain, but this was not a small fire. She broke into a run.

The town had erupted with frenzy. Buildings burst with fire; flames leapt from gaping windows. She stumbled into someone.

"What has happened?" Crissy clutched the jacket of a farmer.

"The mayor went mad. He managed to set four of the buildings on fire before they brought him down."

"Brought him down?"

The man pointed to something in the road. Crissy covered her mouth. The mayor's head had been bashed and his blood oozed into the dirt.

Home. Crissy skirted the body and ran.

Flames ate at the timber and through the shingled roof. The emptiness that had marked her journey out of the woods melted in an instant. Anguish took hold. A scream gurgled in her throat. She raced toward the building, but someone grabbed her around the waist. She struggled against the strong arms holding her, and she was lifted into the air, her feet kicking at nothing.

"No one is in the house. Your family is safe." That voice. His voice. His arms around her. She felt sick.

"Crissy," Sorsha cried, and then soft, familiar arms took hold of her. Another man, Oleg, his arms held her as well. Wolf released her. The other two gushed, speaking words that could not register. The house, her house. Her things. Burning in fire. Destroyed. All her plans frayed to nothing.

She grabbed at her parents. "The chest beneath my bed. I must… Sabine mustn't…" Fire roared behind her. There would be no going inside. No walking the hallways, running her fingers along the wooden banister. The book would be destroyed. Her hold on Sabine would be destroyed. She pushed away from her parents, staring at them, at the fire, at the stranger. She opened her mouth, but words refused to be spoken. She turned and ran.

"What have you done?" Sorsha's scream didn't stop Crissy.

This time she took the path to the ancient house. Sabine must not escape. They could never know what had happened. Rocks cut into her feet, but it didn't matter. Shadows were coming. She could feel them, sense them among the trees. She raced, her lungs on fire.

The clearing was as she remembered. Her labored breath the only noise. She looked at the house. The door stood open. The windows too. Light blue curtains moved in a breeze. The old woman shuffled past the doorway. Hysteria nearly bent Crissy double.

"Grandmother," her voice sounded weak. She fell to her knees and tried again. "Grandmother?"

Her call moved across the clearing. The old woman shuffled back to the doorway. Crissy stood. They stared at each other. Crissy dragged air into her body as she continued to look at what her sister had become. Bent with age, skin that looked like melting wax. Clear brown eyes. She had no trouble seeing them. Knowing that the old woman somehow knew.

Then those familiar eyes widened, the frail body staggered back. The hair on Crissy's nape stood. She turned, slowly moving her body. A wolf stood twenty feet from her. Its lips had curled back, its ears laid flat. Something she had yet to feel coursed through her body. They were magnificent. Larger, stronger, bold. Beautiful. Deadly. She felt fear. Saw death in their eyes. The bag in the beast's mouth dropped to the ground and rolled. Crissy suddenly realized her mistake. Two years in her wardrobe. Among her things. Her room. Her scent permeated and polluted, what should have drawn them to Sabine.

"Crissy."

She dared not take her eyes from the wolves, but she recognized Wolf's voice.

"Remain still." He moved into her periphery.

He was a dead man as well. Did he not realize? Her hope was the house. With Sabine, ironically. Perhaps the spell would hold. She moved her right foot backward, toe on the ground first, and then the heel. She shifted her weight to her right foot. Animal ears perked and settled once more.

"Crissy, don't."

His warning came too late. A flash of gray, and something hit her body. Not from the front, as she had expected, but from the side. She rolled to the ground, getting tangled in her red cape. The heavy material protected her for a moment. But the teeth could not be held back. Her arms were pinned beneath her. She screamed as pain tore through her shoulder. She rolled, but heavy bodies trapped her beneath them. They were trying for her neck, tearing at her face. Ribs cracked beneath the force of their attack. The coppery smell of blood thickened around her. She screamed until a blanket of darkness tore the life out of her.

~

Wolf chased after Crissy. The red cloak flew behind her like a bloody shadow. Madness quickened her pace and he struggled to keep close enough to mark her way. Then he recognized the curve of the path. This is what he had missed. She raced for her grandmother's house? What purpose would drive her in that direction? A cold shiver alerted him to danger.

The pack tracked them. Tracked her. He slowed, pulling his crossbow from its holster. He did not follow her into the clearing. He stopped with his back against a tree, able to watch Crissy and the scene about to play out.

He pulled an arrow into place and held his finger against the trigger. He watched. The old woman came to the door. He had dreamed of her. Of a young woman as well. He searched the windows but saw no sign of the girl.

His senses alerted him to the presence of wolves. He turned his focus. Shadows played among the trees, and he couldn't count their number. Three came toward her from behind. What? Something red dropped from the mouth of one of them. The animals were impressive, large, and robust. Deadlier than he had ever encountered.

Her body tensed for flight. Don't, that would bring them on her. He stepped from his position into the open. "Crissy, remain still." He slowed his motions, not wanting to startle any of the beasts. She moved her foot. No. Then he noticed the skulking fiend on the far side of the clearing. Crissy wouldn't have seen it, and yet, with her position between him and the wolf, he couldn't get a clean shot. Life be cursed, he ran, but the animal reached her first.

Her screams filled the quiet. He pulled the trigger, and managed to wound one of them, but rather than scaring it from its prey, it maddened its attack. Crissy writhed on the ground; darker crimson soaked into the red wool. His focus shifted as a wolf circled him. There wasn't time to load the arrow, but he wasn't as helpless as Crissy had been. He struck out with his weapon, the whimper of the injured animal brought little satisfaction as he was forced to the ground. He rolled onto his back, capturing the snarling jaws in his hands before a mortal wound could be placed. Claws tore at his chest, and he cried out. The jaws clenched together, and he felt fangs digging into his fingers. Weakness pulled at him.

Thunder shattered the woods, and a burst of light flew through the air. The creature fighting him froze. Its size diminished, and with a yelp of fear, it pulled away. Patrick's arms fell to his side. Pain radiated through his body, and he tensed for another attack. Something brushed against his head, and then cool hands touched his cheeks; ran across his forehead. He blinked. Could his eyes deceive him? The young woman of whom he had dreamt knelt beside him. He tried to draw breath to speak, but his chest erupted with pain. He gasped. She moved to his side. Wolf closed his eyes. He felt her spread his shirt, and then agony as she pressed something against his chest.

He gasped for breath, and she brushed a hand across his forehead.

"I am sorry." The same voice as in his dreams. "You are badly wounded. We must stop the flow of blood."

He swallowed. It hurt, but there was no death rattle yet. He forced his eyes open and lifted his hand to brush against her face. Though he left a smear of red across her cheek, she was real. His dream had come to life.

"Who are you?" His voice sounded rough. He covered her hand on his chest, tightened his muscles, and forced himself to sit up. Black swirls washed across his vision. He closed his eyes, drew a shallow breath, and waited for the wave of pain to pass. She gasped, wrapped an arm around his shoulders, and pulled him against her. Another wave of pain radiated through him, but he remained alert.

"Who are you?" Had she answered his questions?

"Sabine. Sabine Bostich."

Her voice sounded tight, hurt. "Are you injured?" He brushed his hand along her side.

She shook her head. "I am well." A sob contradicted her words. "Is she…"

He realized her attention was on Crissy. The red cape covered the body, though obviously stained with blood. "I fear it is so."

The woman, Sabine, cried. Her head pressed against his shoulder. He felt compelled to press his lips against her hair, though movement did not come easily. "You knew her?"

He felt her nod. "She is my sister."

Thunder rumbled overhead. "We should get into the house."

"No." Sabine stiffened. "I will not return to that place."

"But your grandmother, she can help with my wounds."

"There is none but I."

"But I saw…"

She moved enough for him to see her face.

Sadness caused a sheen of tears in her eyes. "You saw me. Cursed to live in the memories of an old woman."

"I dreamt," he shook his head. It wasn't possible. "What has happened to the old woman?"

"I am free of her." She covered her mouth as tears coursed down her cheeks.

"Help me stand." None of it made sense. The wolves and their odd behavior. Crissy, mysterious and dark. Sabine and the old woman were the same person?

Darkness washed over him, and his legs threatened to buckle. Sabine's arm around his waist kept him up. The girl was strong. He looked down at her. Young woman.

Lightning flared, thunder followed, and then steady rain began to fall. "Can we not take refuge during the storm?"

She shook her head. He knew better than to ask a third time.

Chapter 15

*M*isery, thy name is Patrick. He swayed, but Sabine helped him remain upright. How far they had traveled he knew not. It took everything to place one foot in front of the other. Agony to be held against her, and yet without her support he would fall. Cold rain soaked them both, possibly numbing the edge from his pain. They made it through the woods onto the trail leading to town.

Rain poured heavily and he could feel her shiver. "We should be close now."

The rain would help put out the fires, but the scent of burnt carried through the air.

"Ho, a hand please." Sabine yelled. Wolf staggered. And then he felt another person lift his arm. They had arrived. He gratefully welcomed the darkness.

~

Sabine stood shivering in the rain as two men carried the injured stranger away. Billows of smoke wafted in the wind. She took a step closer. Crissy. A sob tore through her, but the pelt of cold rain washed any trace of tears from her face. What had her sister done? Why? Anguish burned inside. What was Sabine to do? Where should she go?

The buildings of Dover looked the same. Familiar faces drifted around her, like shadows from a distant dream. There were voices crying out, but she couldn't understand, her ears seemed filled with the roar of the storm. Someone grabbed her. Thick hands taking hold of her arms. That face— her heart had cried to see him once more, wrapped safe in his embrace. "Father." His name tore from her parched throat. She was home, time to let darkness drag her away for a short while.

~

"We thought fever would take you." Mother gripped Sabine's hand, as Father stood over her shoulder. His face shone with joy, though sadness rimmed his eyes.

Sabine accepted a drink of water and rested her head back on the pillow with a sigh. "How long was I gone?"

"Two years." Mother kissed her hand. "Your father never gave up hope."

Memories faded like shadows dispersed by the light of day. She had the impression of trees, a bench looking out the back door into a garden, and a red cape. "I don't remember what happened. It's as if I were lost in the woods."

"They found your sister in the woods." Tears welled in Mother's eyes. "They say she was the last victim of the wolves. More than a week has passed, and the animals remain hidden."

Oleg crouched beside them, one hand holding his wife, the other holding his daughter. "Let us go to London. Start fresh. I have contacts near London Bridge that can lead to a job. Salvage what we can from the ruins of the house."

"No." Sabine squeezed his hand, her heart thudding unpleasantly. "Nothing from the house. It is what Crissy wanted all along. Let her and that place rest together."

"But there may be treasures among the ruins." Sorsha said. She didn't understand.

Neither did Sabine, but she knew with certainty, the ruins needed to remain undisturbed. "Please, I beg. A fresh start in London. Take nothing from here with us, save each other."

They sensed her agitation, smoothing her forehead with a gentle touch. "As you wish." Oleg smiled as though he could deny her nothing. They needed each other, that was all. Tiredness wound through her body, and she drifted to sleep.

~

The hollow where grandmother's house had been, was cleared. Though the outline of gardens remained, no house stood, no blood marred the earth. Sabine stood in the middle, where the trees parted and allowed sunlight to float down. She twirled.

"You are much the way I first saw you, and yet different." Wolf's voice surrounded her, and she slowed to a stop.

"You're here."

He moved closer. "Our dreams want us together."

Sabine's cheeks flamed. Why would a man want an unschooled... what was she? On the verge of eighteen yet never having lived? She changed the subject. "How do your injuries heal?"

"Sore. But I survive thanks to you. I'm in London to recover at the hospital of St. Katherine."

"Father is moving us to London. Somewhere near the bridge, I think."

He stepped close enough to touch her, and the feel of his finger on her cheek caused her heart to flare. "I will be sure to find you before returning to Ireland."

She wanted him to. Something akin to hope bubbled within. She hadn't thought to ever smile again, and yet her lips twitched with genuine pleasure. His glance at her lips started a fire. He leaned in and kissed her. It didn't matter she was young, or that the mind of an old woman had aged her beyond her years. It mattered kissing him filled her with purpose. He would find her in London. Pursue her for his future. The promise shining in his eyes was that next time, their first time beyond dreams, would be more than either of them could hope for.

The Ugly Duckling

A Princess Fairytale

The Ugly Duckling was first written by Hans Christian Anderson way back in 1844. The tale written by Anderson tells about the woes of a bird who was thought to be one thing, and horribly mistreated because of it, but turns out he was a different bird altogether. This fairytale is nothing like that, and yet, something in it brings the idea of the Ugly Duckling to mind. It is a fun story involving a princess, a curse, a dragon, and a mysterious protector.

Happy reading.

Chapter 1

Soft light passed through the drawn brocade curtains of the queen's bedchamber to fall across the infant in her arms. Queen Stephanalia felt her chest tighten as she stared at the face of her daughter. "What happened? What's wrong with the princess?" She held her hours-old daughter close as she tried to push through the haze of tiredness brought on by giving birth.

Lady Beatrice, the queen's sister, hushed her. "It is your fault. You forgot to set wards against the dark faeries."

Stephanalia shook her head. "Of course, I set them," she protested, but doubts washed over her. She'd been sick for weeks.

Lady Beatrice brushed her hand against Stephanalia's forehead before touching the baby. "You mustn't let anyone know. She would be given over to the wilds if they knew about the curses." Her eyes filled with tears. "The king could order you killed."

Stephanalia wanted to thrust her sister away from the bed, but she was too weak. She blinked moisture from her eyes as she gazed at her daughter.

She'd been perfect. She'd seen her. But now, the tiny face was marred by reddish blemishes and her features look to have been stretched. The pale blue eyes that watched her knew nothing of the ugliness laid upon her. Her mother's heart cried for what had been done, but it changed nothing of how she felt about her baby.

"Let me take her. You need sleep." Lady Beatrice wrapped her hands around the little bundle.

Stephanalia tried to twist away from her. "No. I want to hold her."

Lady Beatrice took her anyway. "There is naught for you to do but sleep."

The queen felt cold fill her as the princess was taken. Her eyes grew heavy. There should have been a way to fight against the curse, but a shadow rose in her mind, and she gave in to sleep.

Chapter 2

Sixteen years later

L ight tumbled across wooden shelves, revealing a wealth of ancient tomes. A breeze of musty air wafted through the library, causing candlelight to flicker. Princess Derylla hunched lower in her seat, praying the curved wood divider would keep her from sight of the others. Voices disturbed the peace of pages scrawled with gall ink.

"She can never be queen. Who wants an ugly duckling for a ruler?"

She bit her lip as the cold voice reached across the shadowy library. Snickering laughs followed the derisive insult. The princess huddled behind the heavy wood desk. She twisted her pale hair around her hand and returned her attention to the open book laid before her. But the words swam. Her heart groaned. She had no more control over the way she looked than any of them. What right did they have to belittle her for things beyond her control?

Flickering sconces caused shadows to ripple across the page. Were more students entering? Or were the girls leaving?

A startled scream from a different part of the library caused her to jump. Something crashed to the floor. A scuffle ensued. Derylla slid from her chair and crouched on the floor. A high-pitched yelp, someone else hollering, and then heavy footsteps. Derylla could see nothing. Her heart hammered more loudly as the steps drew closer. Someone halted next to her hiding place. A burly hand yanked her from beneath the desk into the open. Strong arms lifted her to her feet. Foul breath blew next to her face. She twisted away. His arm tightened around her waist and pulled her against his thick-muscled body.

"Trouble, m'lady, and you be hurt." His voice rasped.

She gasped as the arm tightened and her feet left the floor. He carried her through the room. The knotted design of floor tiles seemed to bounce, causing her stomach to roll. Fear stole her breath. Her feet kicked the door as they passed into the outer hall. The pale afternoon sun lit stained-glass windows. Someone held the door. In a moment, the princess found herself outside.

An iron carriage waited. Another student railed against a captor, her skirts flailing. Derylla felt herself tossed. Light faded as she entered the carriage. She landed among a pile of bodies. Their arms and legs kicked against her, until they all managed to scramble out of the way. Panting breath and a brief glimpse of the prisoners, and then the door slammed shut, leaving them in darkness. Horses pulled forward. Derylla felt herself roll back. She cried out as a foot landed against her side.

Their prison lurched again. Her back hit the side of the wagon. She fell over onto someone else. Arms pushed her away. "Get off me, oaf." The sharp voice laced with fear cut nearly as sharply as the fist that pounded against her arm. Derylla backed as best she could, her legs tangling in her skirts. Someone else, to her left, pushed back.

"This is your fault." The tear-laden accusation hurled through the darkness.

Derylla started. "My fault? How?"

"I have no time for this." The young girl hissed. "The Quagger ball is two days hence."

The conveyance slowed. Everyone silenced. Derylla watched the door as the latch clicked. Low light filled the space. She saw five other students. Gayla's curls bounced as she glared. Rosetta and Gertrude looked equally hateful. Derylla did not recognize the two boys.

A shadow fell across the opening. Someone stood without. "Exit the carriage. Orderly and without fuss. Try to run and you'll discover what a brick against the back of your head feels like." A large man stood near the door. Another man held a rock in his beefy hand. The prisoners began to scoot. Derylla yelped as a hard heel pressed into her hand. Gayla gave her a haughty glare edged with fear. Hand throbbing, Derylla followed. She stumbled off the end of the cart. An unfamiliar hand caught her and pulled her to her feet. She jerked away from him. The third captor was slimmer than the other two. Dark hair fell in waves to his collar and a stubbly beard covered the bottom portion of his face. His eyes gleamed. But then a harsh grip on her chin drew her attention away from him.

A different man held her firmly. His olive skin marked him as a foreigner. The glint of evil shining in his sable-colored eyes made her stomach twist. She tried to pull away, but his grip tightened. "There was only supposed to be the one. Mind explaining why you brought six?" He kept Derylla's chin in his grasp as he glared at the other captors.

The larger man shrugged. "They were all in the library."

"You best find out who they are and what we can get for them."

Derylla tried to pull away, but his fingers tightened painfully. "Going somewhere?" His grin was not friendly. He twisted her head from side to side. "I had not taken much stock in the rumors, but I see they told truth." The accent did not mask his snarl. The husky tone of his voice made him that much fiercer.

Derylla knew what he saw. Eyes too far apart. Crooked nose. Flat lips. Skin the color of wheat and hair barely a shade lighter. She knew what she was, but why did he care?

His lip curled. "Not sure the king will pay to have this one back. We will be lucky to be rid of her."

Derylla narrowed her eyes, anger mixing with fear. "Paid or not, your necks will still crack in the hangman's noose."

"Well now, the girl's got a bit of fire in her." His fist flew toward her face, but the other man stopped him, the sound of flesh against flesh loud in the clearing.

"We'll all be better off if she is unharmed. Do not allow her quick tongue to rile you."

The leader dropped his hand, but his eyes filled with malice. Derylla swallowed as he continued to stare at her. "Get the names of the others."

Derylla glanced at the scared group of students. Attending the same college as the princess was their only crime. She breathed in courage. "If I am your prize, let them go." Her voice sounded small, but the leader seemed surprised to hear it.

"Take care, my lady. No young whelp will protect you from a lashing if my heart is set upon it."

She looked at the outlaw. "I will stay if you release them."

His laugh chilled her. He pushed her away. "Like you have a choice." He pointed at the burly captor. "Did you get names?" At his nod, the man grinned, though there was nothing friendly or comforting about it. "Find an administrator at the university. Double the amount we discussed." He pushed Derylla from him and motioned to the others. "Return them to the wagon cart." His order rang with contempt.

Burly hands gripped her once more and she felt herself shoved backwards, stumbling over her feet. Someone caught her before she fell. The younger man steadied her. His smooth hand squeezing hers as he helped her into the cart. She glimpsed the other five huddled together at the front before the door closed. Derylla set herself in the back corner, using the two walls to steady herself as the vehicle lurched into motion once more.

Chapter 3

H unger gnawed at her as night slid through the slats of the carriage. Chilling air kept goose bumps on her flesh even as the rocking motion of wheels bounced her between the sides of the corner. They continued on. She could hear the others talking softly, huddling together for warmth.

Rumbling of the wheels grew more pronounced as they left the main road. The vehicle lurched to the left, eliciting gasps from them all. They continued for some time across the uneven path. Princess Derylla bent closer to the floor, trying to protect herself from the abuse of ramming her shoulders into the walls of the carriage.

Movement slowed until the carriage stopped completely. It rocked from side to side as men jumped from their perch. Derylla listened as their boots scuffled rocks. The door screeched, though the dark night seemed barely lighter than the inside of their prison.

"There are six of you. And six of you will enter the house. If I have to go into the dark to find ye, you'll be a sorry lot."

A hand grasped her ankle and pulled her forward, her palm scraping against the wood floor. Derylla yelped and would have tumbled to the ground if a strong set of arms hadn't caught her. His breath wasn't rancid as the others, but she shoved him away, wrapping her arms around her body to control the shaking.

"This way, princess." He placed a hand against the back of her neck and pressed her in the direction he wanted to travel. She could not shake his firm grip, and the warmth of his flesh against hers eased the shivers of fear. Ridiculous. He was as much an enemy as the others. She lifted her skirt a bit and stomped across the ground. The darker shape of the house loomed before them. A slim light flickered, then grew as someone lit a lantern. Light spilled through the openings.

Derylla looked up. More than a house. An old keep. "Why have you brought us here?"

"Questions are not for you to be asking, princess. Stay quiet, and ill will not befall you."

"Stay quiet? You expect us to meekly accept our fate?"

"Princess, I beg you, for your sake. He will not hesitate to make your stay even more unpleasant. Guard your tongue. If not for yourself, then for the others."

"I tried to free them."

"Michaels' greed is too great for that. I will protect you as I can, but you must help."

"Protect?" Her hands fisted. "Your will is to receive a share of the ransom. What do you hope to gain by friending me? A stay of execution? No such fortune will befall you." Derylla fought the urge to cry. Tears would be a weakness that cost her. The shadowy figure at her side remained silent. They entered the building.

In a moment, the other five prisoners stumbled across the threshold, along with their jailors. Four men present. The tallest man, the olive-toned foreigner, carried a cane. Cold seeped through the room as he glanced at each of them, lingering on her, his gray eyes eerie. The others felt it as well, slipping closer together. The large, burly man who had carried her from the library cracked a mug against the wood table and lifted a jug. A brown liquid spilled into the cup. He downed it with relish. He poured a second. The third man, almost as wide as he was tall, pulled a seat near the window and sat. Wood creaked but held. Derylla glanced at the fourth. He seemed softer, and yet just as determined. His hair had been tied back, revealing a lean face with high cheeks. His eyes were dark, though she could not discern their color. One of his brows rose. She felt heat flush her face. She turned away.

"Two chambers are prepared. Ladies will take the room at the top of the first flight of stairs, gents you have the room at the second flight. I was not expecting a large catch, you will share what is available."

Derylla looked at the other girls. Share? Not likely. She faced her captor. "What of light? May we have a lantern? Or a candlestick?"

He moved swiftly, inches from her in barely a second. "Light I can grant you. But any thought of escape. Any attempt to attack us, and you will feel the brunt of my anger. I would delight to tear your flesh from your bones. From their bones." He looked at the other three girls.

She swallowed, hoping he would not see her tremble. "This will be resolved soon enough. No need to incur your wrath."

"You think you know things, my lady." His eyes sparked with knowledge. He took a step back. The distance did not ease her fear.

"I will take them." The kindest of them lit another lamp and held it aloft.

With a small grin, the leader dismissed her. Derylla spun on her heel and almost raced across the room. Her skin crawled.

The room he led them to was larger than expected, with slender windows through which none of them would fit. The moment he left, Gayla, Rosetta, and Gertrude pounced on the pile of covers and set a bed near the windows. A knock sounded on the door and the kind stranger opened it. He held an armful of blankets. He offered them to her, sliding a glance at the other three.

Derylla lowered her voice. "They are frightened."

"Did they behave better among the lecture halls of University?"

No. but she couldn't admit it. Not to him. Not here.

"Try to sleep, princess. You will need your strength." The door closed with a firm click, and then something slid over and locked into place.

Derylla pushed against the door, but it held fast.

They were locked in the room.

Chapter 4

Derylla gasped as something sharp connected with her arm. She rolled onto her side and squinted through the pale light in the bedchamber. Rosetta stood beside her pallet.

"Are you mad?" She rubbed her arm. It hurt.

"It is your fault we are here." Rosetta's voice wobbled with emotion.

"How can it be my fault?" Anger surged, the unfairness of it. What gave her the right to judge? "I had no knowledge of their plan. I would gladly have warned you out of the library had I known."

"It is your fault." Rosetta's curls bounced as she swung her head. "This wouldn't have happened if you were as a princess ought to be."

"Will you call me ugly to my face?" Derylla jumped to her feet, felt her eyes burning. She no longer cared. "Do you really think I chose to look this way? That I somehow placed my own eyes too far apart, my lips too wide and narrow?"

"It is not merely your looks." Rosetta's foot pounded on the floor. "You traverse campus with no thought to bodyguards. Had they been present in the library, we would not be here."

"I have no idea what you think I have to do with it. I will gladly plead your case now and again, and if our captors choose to acquiesce, I will rejoice in your freedom. Until such a time, refrain from taking your fear and frustration out on me. I am not, nor ever will be, someone's punching post."

The lock slid and the great door creaked as it pushed open. Derylla whirled. The wide fellow grinned at them.

"Lively this morning, are ya? I reckon you can take it downstairs and put that fight into a decent meal. There are a few provisions in the kitchen."

"The kitchen?" Rosetta stepped forward. "Are you daft? Do you take us for maids? Scullers?"

"I'll take you farther than you want to go if you sass and make a fuss." He stepped through the door, one side of his lip curled up in a snarl.

Derylla stepped into his path, looking at Rosetta. "I am certain with the four of us we can manage a decent meal." She lowered her voice. "Do you want the likes of him, or the others, preparing your breakfast?"

"I am not stepping into the kitchen." Rosetta hissed, but then shifted her eyes toward the large man and back to Derylla.

"We will manage." Derylla spoke firmly. She faced each of the girls. Rosetta huffed but remained silent. Gertrude chewed her bottom lip as she glanced up from her place on the floor. Gayla crossed her arms but said nothing. Derylla returned her attention to their captor. "If you will allow us access to water to refresh ourselves, we will do our best to prepare a breakfast."

"Of course, you will. Do I look like I give you a choice?" He laughed, and spun through the doorway, leaving it open.

Derylla peaked into the hallway. The others stood close behind her. With little light available, she made her way across the fading carpet until she found a set of stairs. They curled around, going up into a tower, and down to the first floor.

"What of Nigel and Osgood? Do you think they are safe?" Gayla whispered.

Derylla didn't bother to respond. She followed the steps to the ground floor and paused. Someone bumped into her from behind.

"There is a bathing house beyond the kitchen gardens."

The girls gasped and several squeaked as the fourth captor turned into the room. Derylla couldn't be sure if she'd made a noise or not, though her chest beat rapidly.

"Go now, together. I primed the pump and drew water into the trough."

"Why?" What did he want? This man with deep eyes held secrets. Derylla shook herself mentally. He was one of them. Charming and alluring in a strange way, but still one of them. Hoping to profit. She raised her chin a notch. The slight widening of his grin revealed his attention. Her nostrils flared. How dare he?

"In which direction is the kitchen?" She kept her voice cold and emotionless.

"Through here." He leaned against the doorpost where they had to pass.

Derylla led the way. Ignoring him, or so she

assured herself.

~

"This water is cold," Gertrude mumbled.

Derylla felt her skin shiver as she pressed her hands beneath the surface and lifted them to her face. It felt brisk. There was no soft towel to remove the droplets before they spoiled her gown. She looked down and grimaced. Sleeping in her gown had spoiled it. How long did they intend them to wear the same clothes?

She took her turn at the loo and led them to the kitchens. A basket with eggs sat on a counter. A loaf of bread was already starting to spoil. Something that looked like meat but smelled like the barn sat beside a cold stove. Derylla pressed her upper front teeth into her lower lip. How did one warm a cold stove?

"Are you going to turn it on?" Rosetta stepped up beside her.

"Do they really think we know such things?" Gertrude joined them.

"They are not a bright bunch. What do you suppose happens to them when they are caught? I am the king's only daughter."

The youngest girl looked confused for a moment, and then her eyes widened, and her mouth spread into a large round shape. "The gallows? Are we worth that much, they risk their lives?"

"I doubt the Michaels fellow considers anyone's neck of much value." Derylla turned to study the stove once more. "We need to get this working."

"I can help."

"Of course, you can. You probably let it go cold

on purpose." She'd been waiting to hear his voice, and he did not disappoint. Derylla turned to face him.

He grinned, looking amused rather than annoyed. "Since I'd rather not settle for burnt eggs or raw meat for breakfast, this is more a help to myself than ingratiating with you."

Derylla breathed in, but the other girls responded before she could cut him down.

"Please, it will be worth taking the chill from the air even before breakfast is prepared."

She tried another tactic. "Where are the others? Osgood and Nigel? What have you done with them?"

"The choice was made to allow you first in the bathing room. Your friends remain locked in their room. Now, may I?" he asked as he stepped closer.

Derylla moved out of the way, setting herself at the counter beside the eggs. She found a bowl, managing to glance toward the stove four times before slamming the stoneware against the counter. The others looked at her, but she ignored them. She picked an egg from the basket and tapped it against the hard surface. She looked, but the egg remained intact. She tapped harder and felt a satisfying crack. She shook the egg above the bowl, but nothing happened. Nothing came out. She looked again. A sliver crossed the surface. She pressed against it, but it didn't budge. She tapped the egg once more on the counter. This time, the shell split open, wet goo running across her fingers. She jerked her hand to the bowl and felt her stomach flop as a glob of yellow slid out of the jagged opening. She scrunched her nose and looked at the bowl. It held raw egg with a piece of shell floating in it. She looked at the rest of the shell in her hand. Was it supposed to go into the bowl as well?

"There is a slop pan for the waste." His voice made her jump and she glared at him. He tilted his head toward the floor. "You don't want the shells. They have nothing for flavor and their crunch is unpleasant."

"You seem to know your way around the kitchen, I should leave you to it." She spun away, but his hand against her arm kept her from moving.

"Remain. The others will not invade this space until the meal is prepared. You are safe here, at least for now."

"You make no sense." Derylla hissed, stepping closer. "Are you enemy or are you friend?" She closed her eyes a moment, foolish question to ask. "What a question. You helped bring us here."

"A path may seem evil and yet stand for a different purpose."

"Who are you? A name."

He grinned but shook his head.

She frowned. "The gallows require no name. You will swing as easily without one at the end of a rope."

"Talk of gallows is unpleasant. Let us focus our attention on eggs."

He left after watching her crack a second egg, this time without adding shell to the mixture. Gone, to stay gone, she hoped. She moved the paddle a touch too hard, and egg slopped over the side of the bowl. He was confusing her on purpose. Irritating her. Challenging her. Helping her. Why? What did he hope to gain? His freedom. He knew they could not succeed. Then why attempt this dangerous plot at so high a price? She glanced toward the empty door. He was a buffer. No, foolishness.

An acrid smell reached her nostrils, and she turned to see smoke pouring from a pan. "Stir, Gertrude." She rushed to the stove, used her skirt to pull the cast iron pan from a burner, and moved the sausage-like meat, scraping at the burnt bottom.

"How am I supposed to know what to do?"

Derylla sighed. "We are trying our best."

A male voice interrupted. "Not good enough, if that is any indication."

Derylla jumped, swirled around. Michaels stared at the pan in her hand. Her wrist ached as he stood silent.

"You are a fool if you expect otherwise. We are ladies, not kitchen help." Rosetta's voice carried across the room. Michaels' eyes darkened as he turned in her direction.

Derylla scooted forward, both hands holding the heavy iron pan as she tried to set it back on the stove and intercept Michaels at the same time.

"Allow us time to finish, sir. It won't be the most elegant meal ever prepared, but it will satisfy."

He turned back to her with an evil gleam. "Do you know what will satisfy?" He wrapped his hand around both of hers. Derylla gasped as he tightened his grip, pushing her fingers painfully into the metal handle. He forced her to the stove, the pot clanging against a burner. She felt heat radiating from the belly of the stove. With a cry, she tried to yank her hands away, but he held her firm.

"Michaels."

The kind man pulled him away, and Derylla yanked her hands from the heat, wrapping them protectively in her skirt. She backed away from the stove.

Michaels roared, grabbing the younger man by the shirt, and slamming him into a wall. "You forget your place."

"I agreed for coin. What purpose is there to harm the girl? To harm any of them?"

"You want that ugly cow reigning over you? Wait, you are foreign. You don't care who leads in the castle."

Michaels moved closer to the other man and his voice dropped. Derylla couldn't hear. A moment later, he glared at her, causing shivers to run up her spine, and then walked out of the room. The other man... his dark look didn't instill fear. She crossed her arms protectively as he stepped closer.

"Are you badly hurt?"

She twisted slightly when he reached for her. "I am unharmed."

"Hurry with breakfast, and then remove yourselves from sight. I know not why he hates you, but he will harm you if he can."

He left, and once again Derylla felt tears gather in her eyes. Who was this man? This caring mercenary?

"If it were spring, we could find valerian root and add it to the pan. That would put an ache in their bellies." Rosetta grumbled as she stepped closer to the stove.

Gertrude thumped a bowl of lumpy dough onto the counter, Gayla close at her side. "Give them a well-done meal and they will think twice before asking us to cook the next meal." Gertrude gave a limp push to the wooden spoon.

Derylla shook her head. "Best we do not draw unwanted attention. Do what we can to appease and wait for help to arrive."

"Is that what you have been taught? Appease the enemy? Wait to be rescued?"

"Mine is not the only life at risk. Stir, for pity's sake." Derylla pushed Gertrude out of the way and carried the mixture of eggs to the stove.

"You'll need a scoop of lard before setting the eggs in the hot pan."

His voice crawled over her like a wave. She closed her eyes, part of her wanting to dump the contents of her bowl into the pan without heeding his advice. Rotten man. She opened her eyes and scowled. "Where?"

His lip twitched, as though he read her thoughts. He motioned to the crock at the back of the stove. She looked at the bowl in her arms. He reached for the spoon, but she backed away a step. Hands held up, palms toward her, he slowly moved one hand forward and took hold of the spoon. Derylla watched as he scooped lard from the crock and dropped it into the pan. The fat sizzled and hissed, sending a woosh of steam into the air. She dumped the contents of her bowl into the pan and stepped back.

"That's one way to do it." He gave her a look

she did not want to interpret. Amusement and something else flickered in his eyes. Cinnamon colored eyes.

She wrapped her arms tightly around the dirty bowl. He glanced from her to the pan with its bubbling contents, then back at her. "You should move the egg in the pan to keep them from burning." He gently pulled the bowl from her grip and held the spoon toward her.

With a huff, she snatched it from his fingers. "Be gone." He must have heard her, but he remained. "Why are you doing this?"

"I cannot reveal that to you, princess. I will protect you as I can, but Michaels' hatred toward you is strong."

"Why? I have done nothing to anger him or call such animosity upon myself." She moved the wooden spoon. Blobs of egg hardened. She scraped along the bottom, thankful nothing black rolled over.

"You are the daughter of kings. Their strength is within you, where he expected only weakness."

His words stirred her heart. He thought she was strong? She fought against the pull of attraction.

"What manner of man is your father? Were you thrown to the street? Is that why you have chosen a lawless path?"

The twinkle in his eye drew her. "No such tragedy, princess. I have lived a life of privilege. I pray you do not ask further of me. I can reveal no more."

She remained focused on the cooking eggs, but felt him move away, the kitchen somehow colder as he exited.

Chapter 5

Derylla stood silent in the opening to the dining hall, watching as the mound of breakfast food dwindled to crumbs. Her own meager fare sat heavy in her stomach. She swallowed, casting her eyes to the tapestry hanging on the wall. Faded colors hid the scene, but there appeared to be trees and an animal leaping over a ditch.

A door banged nearby, causing her to jump. The four men at the table froze. Michaels slowly lowered the mug of ale in his hand as a fifth man stumbled into the room. His breath pulled heavily at his chest. Derylla covered her nose as the scent of horse and unwashed body filled the air. The man bent over Michaels, whispering in his ear. He handed him an envelope. Fear soured her stomach further, but she straightened, mentally shaking herself. Cowering would do no good.

Michaels was educated enough to read, and his cold eyes as he glanced over the parchment at her caused shivers to crawl over her skin. He crumpled the paper, his eyes never leaving hers. Hatred burned in them. But why? Why hate her?

"Lock them in their room. I have preparations to make." He stood and left the room through a different hallway.

The large man lifted a hunk of sausage and tore a bite from it. The kind man rose and walked to her side. "It would be best for all of you to remain out of sight."

"What did the letter say?"

"I did not see it."

A ruckus ensued behind them. Derylla glanced around him. The newest man had grabbed something from the table and the large man had knocked him onto the floor. A plate crashed with him.

"Come on." He pressed a gentle hand against her shoulder and propelled her through the hallway to the kitchen. The other girls turned toward them as they entered. His hand was warm, and she shouldn't be thinking or noticing. She shrugged him off.

The pile of dishes in the sink hadn't moved.

"Don't worry about those. Let's get you to your room."

Derylla followed the others up the spiral staircase to the first landing. Before long, they were locked within their room once more.

"You said there was a letter? What did it say?" Gayla settled on a pile of blankets.

Derylla shrugged. "Michaels did not share. His look was not pleased. It could not have been good news."

"Our fathers will have followed the messenger. Even now, rescue is at hand." Rosetta rushed to the window.

"There is little doubt. The question is what will they do with us before they arrive?"

Three pairs of eyes glared at Derylla. She grimaced and sat on the floor, leaning against a wall. What did it benefit, not facing potential danger? She could not do it alone, but surely the four of them… nothing remained in the room that could be wielded as a weapon. Unless one threw a blanket over the enemy. And him? Would she fight him? Weariness tugged at her. She closed her eyes, leaning her head back.

The door slammed open, and she jerked to her feet. Time had passed. Light through the room looked different. She blinked as the other girls crowded closer to her. Michaels stood in the shadowy opening of the door.

"Get them to the roof." He ordered, then moved. The large man and the wiry drunk surged into the room.

The roof? Fear tugged at her, but Derylla moved with the others. Harsh hands pushed her through the stairwell door. She tripped on the first step, pain radiating through her knee.

"Get up."

Rough hands pulled her to her feet. She began to climb. The narrow steps curved along an outer wall of the keep. The eight of them spread out, the larger man unable to climb as quickly as the others. A hand over her mouth covered her gasp as she was drawn into a dark alcove. Derylla felt herself pressed against someone as she watched the others clamber up the stairs. She didn't need to hear the sound of his voice. Fear faded. She allowed a moment's weakness to lean into him. His hand moved from her mouth and his arms encased her.

"Follow me." He whispered as he released her and then found her hand. He slipped through a thin opening into blackness. Derylla felt a door swoosh closed behind her. She heard a hiss, and then a flicker of light broke the dark. They stood in a hallway.

"A secret passage?" Cobwebs and dirt caused her to shudder, but she kept hold of his hand. He lifted a lantern with his other.

Silence surrounded them as they walked. The passage seemed to angle downward.

"Why do you separate me from the others?"

"He means to kill you. The letter directed him to do so." He stopped, and Derylla bounced into his back. He turned and steadied her. "Soldiers have come. He meant to throw you from the roof before releasing the others."

"But why? What harm have I done?"

"He's been paid to rid the world of you, princess."

"Why? I am nothing. No one."

But suddenly she felt like someone. He pulled her close and touched his lips to hers. Warmth flooded her veins. Her mind faltered as he pulled away. She could only stare. His hand caressed her cheek, and she knew she could not bear harm coming to him.

"Stay here. I will find my way to the soldiers without you."

"No matter what may come, I could never abandon you." His voice sounded husky with emotion. Derylla pushed him away.

"The consequences are too great. Soldiers will take you. You will be imprisoned, most likely hung."

He kissed her once more, eliciting a squeak of surprise. "God will protect me." He pulled her forward.

She tried to stop him, but he refused to let go, his hand firmly gripping her own. Tears wet her cheeks by the time they exited the secret passage and made their way into the courtyard.

Chapter 6

Derylla paused in her traverse across her room to stare at the touch of light against the eastern horizon. Morning. The ache of her feet meant little to the confusion in her mind. Where was he? Were they treating him fairly? Why did she care? She covered her eyes for a moment and gritted her teeth. This was why he had behaved as he did. He wanted her to be confused. She opened her eyes once more and glared at the brightening sky.

"I shan't do it. I won't interfere." The room remained silent, though a faraway screech of an owl beyond the window beckoned dawn. "He deserves his fate, as they all do." Her voice broke no argument, but her mind faltered. He'd kissed her with no sign of revulsion in his expression. Kindness? Caring?

With a groan, she resumed pacing. He meant her to intercede. Every action, every word had pulled at her. Foolish, this desire to beg mercy of her father. She stopped at the mirror. How could he look upon her and not revile her image? Her own stomach flopped, twisting as it ever did. She pressed her hands against her cheeks. Her eyes remained fixed, too far from her nose. She dropped her hands to her sides.

His had been an act. There could be no other explanation. She sighed and turned from the gilded reflection. What of it? Even if he had lied, eloquently and masterfully, he made her feel what? Her feet resumed, following the edge of the carpet from the double doors of the closet to the picture window then a slight turn to the main bedroom door. Spin on her heel and back again.

She would do it. She would request of her father a show of pity. The kind criminal had earned it.

~

Breakfast hadn't been possible. Derylla barely managed a few sips of warmed chocolate and a glass of juice. She donned her white day dress with ivory trim. The light color made her own skin seem not quite as pale. The skirt flowed about her. Her nervous fingers twittered with the folds.

She stood before the door of the king's morning room. He would be perched behind the massive dark oak desk, papers and books piled around him. A dog would lounge on the floor at his feet, its tail thumping once it saw her. She took a breath and raised her hand to knock. He would grant her request. He should. Anyway. A mumbled grunt sounded from the other side of the door, and she pushed it open.

Light from windows on two walls provided the necessary means for paperwork. The king sat, much as she had envisioned. He had yet to don his royal robes, but his silver hair, high brows, and firm features marked him as one of importance. His dark eyes focused on her. She gulped.

"You are well this morning, daughter?" His voice filled the room.

Derylla smiled. He loved her, this she knew, even if she wasn't the son he needed or the beauty he would have desired. "I have recovered nicely."

He tapped a pile of papers at his elbow. "No fear these men will beleaguer you ever again. I am signing their death warrants."

Derylla pressed her hand against her throat. "That is the reason I seek you this morning. Doubtless, the captain of the guard told you I was saved by one of the men. He brought me to them, rather than allow their leader to take me to the roof."

He lifted the page in front of him. "The younger man with tawny hair. Refused to provide his name for the death warrant. But it matters not."

"Father, no." Derylla placed her hand against his arm to stop him from signing the document. "He saved my life. He protected me from harm. Surely that should spare his life!"

"He was every bit as guilty as the others. Any kindness was done for precisely this purpose."

"You are wrong. Please, I beg you this favor." Derylla didn't stop tears from flowing down her cheeks.

"I cannot." The king moved her hand. His quill marked the document, sealing the fate of the youngest kidnapper. Five men in total, condemned to death for crimes against the crown.

~

Derylla pulled her cloak close as she slumped through the shadows in the dungeon. She found him in a corner. His chains rattled as he turned in her direction.

"You shouldn't be here, Princess."

His voice sounded weary.

She pressed a leather bag of water into his hand. "Drink."

He accepted, draining the pouch. He dropped his hand to his lap with a sigh of contentment. He tilted his head in her direction. "I still will not reveal my name, Princess."

She had to smile at his tenacity. "But your family. Will they not wonder?" She broke a piece of bread with raisins and mince from the loaf hidden beneath her cloak. She held her hand close enough for him to reach for it.

He accepted the bread, and then pulled her hand to his lips, kissing the calloused skin of her palm. "I did as I ought to have done. I believe God will change my fate." He gave her a stern look. "Without your help."

Derylla, flustered by his touch, rubbed her hand against the rough fabric of her cloak. "You are a stubborn man."

"And you are a beautiful woman. In your heart, where time will never cause it to fade away."

She swallowed, trying to ease the thickening of her throat as she pulled another piece of bread and gave it to him. "Why continue your charade? The warrant has been signed." She looked at the package in the folds of her skirt, unable to face him. "I tried. For the kindness you showed, I tried to stay the king's hand, but he has signed your death warrant. Your acting has availed you nothing." She looked up once more. "I warned you it would not."

His low laugh brought bumps to her skin. "I did as I felt led to do."

"You will die. Why not explain yourself?"

"Your father may order death, but it is God who gives and takes. The story will not end here. Go, my lady. This is not a place for you. But be cautious. Michaels destroyed the letter before anyone could find it, but someone in the castle wishes you harm. Your enemies are not all residents among the chains."

She shivered as she placed the remaining bread within his grasp. "I will bring more water later."

"No."

She offered a tiny smile. "You are not the only stubborn one, sir."

Chapter 7

The halls filled with commotion, but Derylla couldn't focus. Two days remained and the prisoners would be executed. The gallows waited, a ready price to pay for their crime. Someone bumped into her. She looked up. A thin man had collapsed on the stone floor. Others mulled about him. Her mind cleared and she rushed to his side. The smell of charred flesh assaulted her nose. Skin along the right side of his face puckered, burnt layers looking more like the melting wax of a candle.

"Call the healer," she ordered. She pushed against his shoulder so he could lay flat. "Bring a blanket." She glanced at the growing crowd. Servants ran to do her bidding, but the others stood, staring in silence. She returned her attention to the injured man, placing her hand against his good cheek. His lips moved, but no sound elicited.

"What is this?" The king's voice charged through the hall. He stood over her.

"I know not. He is gravely wounded. Burned."

A hand reached to grab her arm. The man's mouth moved. "Dragon."

Her father crouched beside her. "What did he say?"

"Dragon. Beyond the vale." His body was gripped in a convulsion, arms and legs stiffening. His hand on her sleeve pulled and she heard the fabric rip. He tried to speak more, but his mouth gaped open. His eyes widened. She gripped his hand. His eyes glazed and light faded from them.

"Remove my daughter." The king pulled her to her feet and pushed her against a servant. She stared at the body of the dead man. "Go now."

She was pulled away.

~

Queen Stephanalia shivered as a shadow crossed her heart. With her daughter safely returned home, she should feel joy. Relief. Yet, her nerves twitched and hummed with unknown causes. The door of her sitting room banged against the wall, causing her to jump from her seat with a sharp cry. Hand against her throat, she turned to the young girl standing in the opening.

Curt words died on her lips as she took in the girl's paleness and wide, fearful eyes. "What has happened?" The queen adjusted her skirts, awaiting an answer.

It took a moment for her to respond. "The king requests that you attend him."

"Is something wrong?"

"A man has died. I am not sure what led him to such a state." The girl shivered.

"Death?" Too long she had expected it, feeling it nip at her heals. What had brought it to them?

What dreaded doom must they face? "Is he in the throne room?"

She shook her head. "He awaits you in the library."

Queen Stephanalia hurried from the room. The door to the library was open when she arrived a few minutes later, panting for breath. She paused in the doorway, hand against her throat, willing her heart to settle.

King William rarely looked anything but put together, yet now he removed his crown, adding it to a large box. He must have heard her, for he turned. He stretched his hand to her.

Queen Stephanalia tightened her hold on a necklace at her throat. "My dear, what has happened? The servant said someone died." She moved closer.

He nodded. "Dragon's breath. Remove any jewelry or precious metals you may have. Take our daughter and flee."

Stephanalia felt her heart thud with fear. "Where do we go?" she asked as she pulled the clasp from her necklace. Gems sparkled in a flash of sunlight before she dropped them into the box.

"Be sure Derylla takes nothing that could draw the dragon's attention."

She nodded. "I will oversee her packing myself." She pulled away, but then grasped his arm. "What will you do?"

"We must find champions to battle the beast. I will be more at ease knowing you and Derylla are safely away."

She nodded. "We can travel to Carrath. That is a

few days' ride from here."

The king closed his eyes for a moment. "Be quick in your preparations. I will find you within an hour to see you off." He squeezed her hand and released her.

Queen Stephanalia would have preferred a sign of affection, but she did not deserve it. She raced towards Derylla's room.

~

"You are not yet packed?" Derylla's mother swept into the room.

Derylla choked back tears. The smell of burnt flesh remained with her.

The queen opened a trunk at the foot of the bed. "We are leaving. Within the hour, if they can settle the carriages."

Derylla stopped pacing the length of the room. "Leaving? For where?"

"We'll go south to Carrath."

"But I can't leave, not now." She had to find a way to save him. Think. What good was a brain if it lacked substance when she needed it most?

"Your father has ordered it."

"Your king orders you." A deeper voice echoed the queen.

Derylla turned her attention as her father entered the room.

"Dragons have but one purpose. Seek treasure. If it is come to our land, it will make its way to the palace and the storehouses beneath us. It will come to destroy, Derylla."

"I will not run."

"You will do as you are bid. The word of the

king is final. I must send men to fight the beast." He quickened his steps to the door. "You there," he waved at a pair of guards in the hall. "Bring the prisoners to the Great Hall."

The prisoners? Why would he want them? She moved to follow him, but someone grabbed her arm. She looked up at her mother.

"You heard the king."

"Priscilla will pack. Tell her where we go, she will know better than I what to bring." She pulled away and followed her father.

He used a side door close to the dais. The prisoners would be forced to walk the length of the room. Derylla hid herself behind a palm as the doors of the Great Hall were flung open. The men were brought in. Chains around their feet clacked louder than the patter of their bare feet across the marble.

The king stepped to his throne as the prisoners were forced to kneel before him. "A plague has come upon us. A dragon from the north. If you wish to save your neck from the hangman's noose, you will find the beast and destroy it."

Michaels' cackle echoed in the huge chamber. "A noose sounds like a kinder end than a dragon's kiss."

"Here there is no hope for you. The rope awaits day after tomorrow."

"I will go."

The king faced the youngest prisoner. Derylla shook her head. What folly did he plan? The king's voice did not sound pleased. "You endear my daughter to you. And now you would find a way to have your freedom."

"God works in mysterious ways."

She watched as a soldier pulled him to his feet.

"I will join him. We all will." Michaels stood as well. The other three hesitated before rising beside him.

The king nodded. "Very well. Defeat the dragon. Bring me proof of your success. And then you will have your freedom from the noose. Betray me and I will hunt you to the ends of the earth."

Derylla recognized the gleam in Michaels' eyes. He meant to murder. "Father, no." She stepped from her hiding place.

His mouth tightened. "You disobey me, girl." He waved to guards on the dais. "Return my daughter to her chamber. Remain at the door. She is not to leave until the carriage is prepared."

"But you must not let them go together."

"Silence, girl." The king stood. Even through his beard she could see the snarl of his lips. "Will you tell the king his business? Do as I say, or you will feel the lash of the whip against your stubborn back."

"Go. I would not have you harmed on my account." Soft words of the prisoner caressed her skin. Derylla had no desire to upset her father further, but what was she to do about the stranger? She ran from the throne room. She could hear the clink of soldiers following close behind.

Chapter 8

W ho will go with you, my lady? What do I pack?" The maid wrung her hands as Derylla separated her hair into three sections and twisted them around each other.

Derylla sat on the trunk that had been prepared. "Do not fret, Priscilla. Is the queen's trunk packed as well?"

The maid nodded.

Derylla finished braiding her hair and looped it around her head. "No jewels? Nothing to snag the dragon's attention?"

Priscilla nodded again.

"Good. Prepare the queen to journey to Abernathy, in Carrath. Get her settled in the carriage." Derylla finished braiding her hair and looped it around her head. "Let them think I am in the other carriage. By the time they realize I am not, I will have caught up with the dragon hunters."

"If you are to catch them, you will need something other than a dress. The wild is no place for soft fabric."

"Had I known this would be happening, I would have had the dressmaker prepare something more appropriate."

Priscilla bit her bottom lip, then seemed to make up her mind about something. "Wait here. I will return in a moment."

The slender girl flew through the doorway. A soldier peeked into the room. Derylla pulled at her skirt. No, the fabric would not survive travel through the brush. She checked the door. Priscilla had been with her for years, but could she be trusted with such a secret? What if she let the soldiers know? What if they kept her from going after them? Drat the man for refusing to tell her his name. The others would most likely kill him once they were far enough removed from the castle.

Priscilla slunk into the room with something draped over her arm. "They belong to Robbie, my brother. He won't mind, seeing how you be the princess and all." She offered them to Derylla.

A set of explorers. Derylla donned the unusual clothes. The pants were made of heavy weave interlocked with leather. She secured them at her waist with a belt. The shirt hung to her thighs, and a leather vest held it in place. She threw on her cloak to ward off the evening chill.

Priscilla chewed on her lower lip as she watched the soldiers lingering near the door. "They're still there."

"Then we put them to use. Ask them to take the luggage to the second carriage. I will remain inside. Send them for Mother's things next and then let them think I already went to the carriage."

Derylla settled at the window seat as the soldiers came into the room. She covered her lap with a quilt to keep them from noticing her strange garb. Priscilla followed them out, leaving Derylla alone in the room. She looked out the window. Daylight was starting to fade. She waited, allowing enough time for the soldiers to pack the carriage and head to the queen's quarters.

Night had come by the time she left the palace for the stables. No one stopped her as she selected a steed and wolf hound.

She knelt beside the hound, pressing a piece of fabric to its muzzle. "Find him."

The hound rumbled deep within its chest and took off into the dark. Derylla jumped onto her horse to follow.

The prisoners had taken the road from the castle into town. Though the hound traveled around a tavern twice, it soon found another trail following the main road away from the town. The hound led her north. Would they seek out the dragon? She hadn't expected it. Night closed around her as the light from town faded. Stars shone overhead and a gibbous moon lit the path. The hound remained closer, allowing her to track easily. A few more miles, and they took a smaller, unpaved road. She slowed her horse to a walk. The hound barked. It had found something.

"No!" She dropped to her knees beside the inert form of her friend. The wolf hound sat at his head. She turned him over, and then unbuttoned his jacket. She laid her head upon his chest. She could hear the beat of his heart. She closed her eyes against the swell of emotion. Moving her hand across his chest and abdomen, she found his wound.

Blood turned her white shirt red as she wiped her hand and went to the saddle bags for supplies.

~

"How?"

"Sh. Don't speak." Derylla changed the dressing on his wound.

His eyes closed. "You do have a talent. You bring life from the grave."

"You speak nonsense." She reprimanded him gently. "God is the only one who gives and takes what is meant to be given and taken."

"I didn't think you believed in God."

"Of course, I do. I just didn't see how he could save you. Dragons never entered my thoughts."

He tried to laugh, but she could see pain in him. His hand touched hers. "I warned you. It would be spectacular."

"Go home." She huffed.

"You are the one going home, Princess." He glared at her. "I am going to hunt dragon."

"You said God saved you. You require time to rest and heal."

"I feel remarkably well." He stretched to prove it.

Derylla turned her head aside. "You can't hunt in the dark. You might as well sleep." Stubborn man.

~

Mists kissed the land as dawn brightened the sky. Derylla turned on her side and stretched her back. The ground was not the thick mattress of her bedchamber. She sighed. Small price to pay for helping him. She heard movement.

45

"What are you doing?" Derylla asked as he stood on shaky legs.

"Preparing for the quest."

"What will you do when you reach the others? Allow them to kill you properly?"

"I gave my word, and I will not yield." He stood in front of her, hands on his hips.

"Then I go with you."

"You return to the palace."

"I will not." She stomped her foot. "I move forward. With or without you."

They stood toe to toe, seething at each other. The wolf hound flipped his head back and forth.

"You are a stubborn woman."

"And you are a wounded man. There is no shame in accepting help."

With a grunt of frustration, he doused the fire and rolled his bed. Derylla prepared to leave, a tiny grin on her face and a lightness to her step. She pulled her horse to a rock where she could mount with ease.

As they journeyed, Derylla felt the horse tense beneath her. It wanted speed. But the young man walked beside her, and she refused to leave him unaided. "Give me a name to call you, even if you will not tell me the truth."

"Nolan." He winced, hand against his side.

She narrowed her eyes. "Are you bleeding?"

"No. Your stiches hold fast."

Mayhap they did, but he hurt. Willful man. "Ride with me"

"Wouldn't be proper."

"Wolf will prevent you from anything

untoward. Nolan." She tried his name. Why did it matter that she was able to call him something? "At this rate, the beast will be killed, and honor given to our enemy."

"Honor will never go to that man. He has none to begin with."

He moved closer to the horse. He probably would not accept help for his own comfort, but his desire to accomplish the goal burned in his eyes.

She held her hand to him. Nolan accepted, placed his foot in the stirrup, and climbed behind her. He settled in place. She signaled the horse to move. Wolf followed.

With his head against her shoulder, she could tell he dozed. But his arm around her waist never slacked. She laced her fingers with his and held the reins with her other hand. No human being, save her parents, had been this close to her. He felt warm and solid, causing her stomach to flutter.

Hours passed. In the distance, mountains seemed to grow from the earth. A hint of fire wafted on the breeze. Derylla nudged Nolan. She felt his arm tighten as he straightened.

"How fairs your side?"

"I am well, your kindness is healing. This land is unfamiliar, where are we?"

"Are you not of the north?" Though she could not see him, his chest rumbled against her back as he spoke.

"I have never been this way. My home lies west."

West? To which country could he refer? "These are the Majestics. Some are solid granite. Others form a series of caves."

"A lair for a dragon, perhaps, that has traveled further than it should?"

She nodded. "Do you smell that?"

"Michaels and his crew may have camped nearby."

"They'd have walked half the night to get this far."

The wolf hound growled. Derylla pulled the horse to a stop. Nolan dropped to the ground, unharmed, she was glad to see. Derylla alighted and she moved the horse to a copse of trees. A sword slipped free of its scabbard as she tugged on the handle. "There is but one sword."

"That is all I require." He reached toward her.

"You?" She pulled away with a frown. "I brought the sword. I'll be using it."

"Your father freed me to kill the dragon. What do you think he will do if his only daughter is harmed in the process?"

"Doesn't matter what he thinks since he isn't here to dictate my actions."

"We can argue the finer points of diplomacy later, your highness." He tried to grab the hilt, but she skipped out of reach. Instead, she pointed the sharp end in his direction.

"You lost your weapon when you allowed yourself to be attacked by Michaels. I will hold the course for now."

"With a tongue as sharp as yours I don't suppose I'll have need for any other weapon."

She wanted to stick her tongue out at him. Insufferable. The ground shook and the seriousness of their predicament surfaced. Her smile swept away. They moved out from the protection of the trees to study the range of mountains closest to them.

He tapped her shoulder and pointed. A man lay sprawled across the grass. The large criminal. They sprinted across the distance. Nolan knelt to turn him over while Derylla searched the shadowy entrance into the caves. He returned to her side and shook his head. Understood. They continued forward without speaking. Light flickered and she looked down. Nolan had taken the dead man's sword. She raised her own, swiping it through the air. The balance felt good.

Nolan stayed her motion with a hand to her wrist. More bodies.

He pulled her aside and stood close enough for her to feel his breath on her cheek as he spoke.

"You remain here. I will enter the caves."

She shook her head. "God brought us together. There will be need for both of us."

"He will smell you first, not only girl, but royal. It is safer for you to remain here."

She placed her hand on his cheek. "I did not travel this far to remain safe."

He pointed at the bodies. "Not safe at all."

"If I can distract him, you can set the kill."

"Your father called you a stubborn woman, did he not?"

"I am not stubborn. I aim to do what is right. We go together."

They lost track of time within the darkness of

the caves. Though firelight burned in the torches, the light did not reach far. Somewhere, a deep soft voice murmured with laughter. A red hue lit the cavern well enough to see the walls, the expanse of space. Though they could not yet see the beast, Derylla felt her blood turn cold. She pushed fear aside. Instead, she tapped Nolan's shoulder and pointed at an outcropping. He pointed at her, but she shook her head. He held up two fingers and distanced them apart. Yes, let the dragon move between them and they could attack on both sides. He pressed a hard kiss to her lips. *Why did he keep doing that*? But the beast was coming, and she could not linger her thoughts in that direction.

"You are of royal blood. I smell it in you." The sound of its voice was both pleasant and terrifying. With a deep rumbling, it spoke words she could understand. How did it learn language?

She gripped the sword tighter. "I am the daughter of kings."

"Daughter?" She could feel its movement through the rock beneath her feet. "Ah, daughter. What sweet savor you offer."

A great shadow moved against the wall. She raised her sword, but it laughed. Its voice chilled the heated room.

"You come against me with iron? Will you not offer yourself to me as a willing sacrifice?"

"Nay. I am here to destroy you. Why have you come?"

"The curses, my child." It hissed, voice pulling at her. "The curses. They draw me from slumber, wake me from dreams. You are bound by a curse."

"Me?" Derylla shook the veil of mesmerism from her mind. "I am no curse."

"Can you not see?" Its breath heated the air. "No. I suppose you cannot."

A brighter glow started in the center of the room. Gleams of light shone upward, to the ceiling of the cavern.

"Will you not look? See what it is that binds you."

Derylla found herself looking into a pool of water. So smooth and clear the water, it was as though she looked into a mirror. She stepped away.

Firey anger swept through her. "It is a lie," her voice reverberated from the rock as she screamed at the vile dragon.

"It is not my nature to lie. You are as you see."

"But my face is not lovely. I look nothing like that image."

"It is the curse that has made you as you appear."

"Curse? Who would put a curse upon me? Why?"

"Who can understand the human mind and what it conceives in its frailty?"

"You care naught for humans. Is that why you have come? You seek to destroy us?"

"I have no purpose to destroy. I was summoned. With you as my prey."

"But by whom?"

"Who will be in your stead?"

"My cousin is too young."

"But his mother is not. And your own mother's sin would prevent her from protecting you."

"Mother?" Derylla dropped her sword, the sound of it striking rock echoed through the vast space.

The dragon's voice drifted closer. "A moment of weakness, she has regretted for an age. But her sister refuses to release her. As she refuses to release you."

"Don't listen to him, Princess. Pick up your weapon!" Nolan's voice reverberated through the emptiness. Derylla shook her head. Dragon's breath washed over her. She reached for the sword. A dragon's scale sliced her hand. She ignored the heat and thrashed out. She felt it slide into flesh. The beast screamed. Something hit her, sending her flying through the air until her body slammed into hardness and she sank into oblivion.

~

Torches flickered throughout the cavern. The body of the beast sprawled across the room. Derylla sat slowly. Her body ached, and the wound on her hand burned. Nolan lifted his sword high and sliced talons from the dragon. He placed them in a leather pouch at his side. She used her sword to leverage herself to her feet. The room spun, but she refused to go down again.

"I've got you." She felt Nolan's arm around her.

"I must have hit my head pretty hard."

She led them back through the maze of caves. Each step seemed like a dream. It might have been days, or mere minutes. Dragon's breath had mesmerized her. How long had they waltzed with words? Even now, the curtain it had draped over her threatened to fall once more. Daylight became apparent, and her feet moved across the rock. Nolan kept pace with her.

Walking into the open seemed oddly bleached of color as they stepped out of the mountain. Derylla looked at the wound on her hand. She felt peculiar.

"Are dragons poisonous?" She held her hand to Nolan and knew no more.

Chapter 9

She woke in a soft bed, fire blazing. Clean covers draped over her body. Her hand and lower arm were wrapped in a bandage.

"You're awake, Miss?"

Derylla turned to Priscilla. "I believe I am."

Priscilla remained a few feet away from the bed.

"What is wrong?" Derylla recognized fear in her maid. "What has happened?"

But Priscilla ran from the room without a word. Derylla tried to sit up but felt too weak to accomplish it on her own. She began to pull at the wrapping around her arm.

"Leave it be." Her mother placed a hand over her own.

She looked up to see tears on her mother's cheeks. "What is it? What has happened?"

"You are changed."

"Am I so horrible now that all are to fear me?" She could hear her own fear. "Help me rise. What has happened? How did I return to the palace? What of my companion, Nolan? Where is he?"

Her mother fumbled, but Derylla managed to swing her legs off the bed.

"Who is Nolan?" Her mother smoothed her own gown before assisting Derylla with hers.

"The man who worked with me to destroy the dragon. The one who protected me from the kidnappers."

"Him? He is imprisoned, due to die on the morrow as he should. Nearly got you killed."

"He saved my life. More than once. Father promised to forgive him." She felt her strength returning.

"There was no proof. When the two of you were found, you were all but dead."

Derylla looked at her wrapped hand. "I must go to him. Speak with him."

"I forbid it."

Derylla stared at her mother. "See to your own sins before you condemn another."

Her mother reeled back as though slapped. Derylla found herself able to stand, and she walked from her bedchamber.

~

"Seems we've been here before, Princess." He accepted her water.

"What happened with the talons. I saw you take them from the dragon."

"The apothecary needed them to counter the dragon's poison. You would have died without them."

Tears pooled in her eyes and dripped down her cheeks. She shook her head. "Where is the apothecary? Why has he not spoken for you?"

"They think tis his work that has changed you."

"What has happened? Did the dragon…" she

touched her cheeks but felt nothing but her usual soft skin. Nolan took her hands.

"You are as your heart has always been. The dragon's poison broke the curse."

"The curse." She sat up. "I must speak to mother. She will stop this." She offered a bright smile, kissed his cheek, and ran from the prison.

~

"How did you know?" Mother remained in the same spot as when Derylla left.

"The dragon revealed the truth. You must tell father, get him to release Nolan."

"I cannot! What would he think of me, allowing a curse to be brought upon his own daughter?"

"Nolan will die, even though he accomplished the challenge. I forgive you, mother. Please, spare his life. For me."

Sobs shook her mother, but she nodded. Sorrow gleamed in her eyes as she stood before Derylla. Though her mouth opened, no words were said. She ran from the room. Derylla waited.

Chapter 10

Queen Stephanalia thought her heart would break into tiny bits and pieces with each step she took down the long marble-floored hallway. "How am I to tell him? How can I not?" She muttered to herself as she walked. It might not have been as hard if her thoughts weren't filled with sweet Derylla's face. Sixteen years the child had suffered because of her mother. She wiped tears from her cheeks.

"You cannot reveal anything."

A voice hissed from a shadowed alcove. Lady Beatrice moved into the light. Any sense of sisterly affection had long since given over to fear. Even now, the sight of Beatrice' cold beauty made Stephanalia's stomach twist, and her chest tighten, locking her breath in her throat.

Stephanalia stopped. "I am going to the king with the truth." Her soft voice could not hide her tremors.

"What truth?" Beatrice glided closer. "You let your daughter be cursed? Allowed her to steep in a curse for years?"

Stephanalia could not deny her hand in

Derylla's fate. In the excitement of being with child, the festivities, the lavish gifts—her head had been turned. Sickness had set upon her and her need to put up wards against ill omens had fallen to the wayside. The dark faerie had left her mark on the infant. Stephanalia allowed the mask to remain, claiming the child had been born to it. She glared at her sister. "I have allowed you to turn my head too often. Living in the palace, raising your son as a prince of the land… Derylla could have been killed."

"The girl is as foolish as her mother." Beatrice waved her hand in dismissal.

"She is not." Stephanalia stood straighter. "Derylla is smart and clever. And brave. She faced a dragon." She narrowed her eyes. "How is it a fire breather of the north comes this far south?"

"The people of this country do not desire the princess to rule over them. She is called the Ugly Duckling."

"They react to a curse. When Derylla is known, she will be loved for who she is. Her looks will not matter." She paused as the truth revealed itself. "Is that why you decided to kill her?"

Beatrice' dark eyes glittered with evil. "The king should have chosen me to be his bride. I would have given him a son. I would take my place as queen and the people would fear me with adoration." She drew a slim dagger from within her coat. "Once the king has fulfilled his widower mourning, I will show him how good a queen I make."

Stephanalia gasped, but a row of soldiers turned

the corner.

"Protect the queen." The king declared.

Beatrice' dagger clattered as it struck the marble. She struggled against the men holding her fast until her arms were wrenched behind her back. She cried out in a pained voice.

Stephanalia stared at the king. *How long had he been near? What had he heard?* What he might or might not know no longer mattered, she could not bear the weight. "It is my fault. I knew a curse had been put upon Derylla shortly after she lay in her bassinette. Had I been willing to admit..." Tears choked her voice.

The king moved toward her. "But Beatrice convinced you to let us think our daughter had been born that way."

"I forgot to hang the wards. I did not protect her as I should. If you knew the truth, I would never be allowed close to my daughter."

"The wards were in place."

"They couldn't be. How else could..." she looked at her sister who struggled against soldiers.

"The dark faerie was invited."

The king spoke but Stephanalia kept her attention on her sister. She shook her head. "You wouldn't do such a thing." The tears in Stephanalia's eyes couldn't hide the hatred blazing in Beatrice.

"You are nothing." Beatrice snarled. "What use do we have for a worthless queen and her ugly daughter?"

The king turned a hard stare on Beatrice. "You hired a foreigner to kidnap the princess and kill her."

Beatrice tossed her head back in an act of defiance. "What does it matter? He failed."

"The dragon? Was that of your devise as well?" The king's voice drew softer.

"Curses have their use. I knew the dragon would be drawn to her."

"Beatrice! The dragon could have laid waste to our country. How could you risk such death and destruction?"

"If the land cannot be saved from the likes of Derylla, what better use than to fuel dragon fire?"

"Lady Beatrice Hongrove, you are convicted of crimes against the crown, for attempting to murder my daughter and my wife, for attempting to wreak havoc on the innocent people of our country. Your neck will be bound in a noose, and you will hang within the hour." The king looked to the captain of the guard. "Make it so."

Beatrice's screams echoed through the hallway until they faded as the soldiers drew her from the palace. Stephanalia held her arms round herself, her body shaking with fear and cold.

"Come." The king stood beside her.

"I am as much to blame as Beatrice. I have earned the same fate."

"Your actions have never come through hate nor greed. She caught you when you were alone at your weakest, made you believe her lies."

She finally looked at him, and the compassion in his eyes made her want to cry. "How can I face Derylla?"

"Do you doubt our daughter will forgive you?"

He wrapped an arm around her shoulder.

Stephanalia rested her head against the strength of his chest. "The man who fought the dragon, will you release him now?"

He nodded. "She cares for him, but such a match cannot take place."

Stephanalia agreed. Derylla would be hurt, but wounds of a broken heart could heal. She closed her eyes, shuddering at the thought of Beatrice's body swinging from the end of a rope. She had to hope the wounds of a broken heart could heal.

The king took her hand and they walked together to the throne room.

Chapter 11

S ilence filled Derylla's chamber in the wake of her mother's exit. Uncertainty gnawed at her, but she sat at her dressing table. She gulped and lifted her eyes to look in the mirror. She gasped at her image. It was the same, yet it seemed as though a warped mirror had been set to right. Her skin looked creamy. Her long hair was the color of autumn leaves. Her eyes were closer to each other, her lips full. She touched her nose. How she could look the same, and yet different. Feel the same, and yet different?

The image at the lake in the dragon's lair had been true. She touched her cheek, moving her head from one side to the other. Almost, she wished her other self to return. What would the people say now? How would they treat her? Only one man made her feel as though her looks hadn't mattered. Mother hadn't returned though several hours had passed. Derylla needed to know Nolan was safe. With a final glance at herself, she pulled away from the mirror to seek out the king.

~

"What has happened? Nolan is gone." Derylla

raced into the council room. The sight of her mother dressed in black staring out a window gave her pause. She looked through the glass and covered her mouth. Aunt Beatrice swung from the gallows.

"Your mother swears she knew nothing of the plan to kill you and inherit the kingdom for her son." The King put his arm around Derylla's shoulder. "Is Nolan the man from the prison?"

She nodded. He pulled her away from the gristly sight. "I released him."

"Truly, Father?" The light of joy shone through her heart as she looked up at him.

"I pardoned his sentence." The king nodded. "He was taken to the edge of the kingdom and forbidden to return."

"Taken…forbidden… but why?"

"He trifled with your safety."

"I do not want him gone."

"You think you care for him, but it matters not. I have forged a contract with a neighboring country, a marriage contract."

"A marriage contract?" She stepped back, shocked.

"It was done long ago, child."

"Who is he?"

"Prince Valanon. By all accounts he is an honorable man. He will protect you, not allow you to be poisoned by dragons or kidnapped by ruffians."

"I know nothing about him. How can I be expected to marry a stranger?"

"Have faith. Give him a chance."

Night had fallen. Derylla returned to her room.

The words of her father continued to echo in her mind. "Give him a chance?" Derylla pounded her pillow, damp with tears. "How can I?" Her heart longed for another.

Chapter 12

Days cooled. Leaves plummeted to the earth, leaving skeletal branches against the crisp blue sky. Word reached the palace of a convoy eight days out. The messenger presented a tiny box.

He bowed, head to the ground with hands raised. "For her highness, the princess."

Derylla unwrapped the gift. She removed the lid and a butterfly fluttered into the air. Her heart flared to life for a moment, but then settled once more into twilight.

Three nights passed, and another gift arrived. A single pendant on a slim cord glittered on a puff of cotton. The drop was precisely the color of dragon scale. The scar on her hand throbbed and she was loath to pick it up.

The third gift arrived the morning of the expected entourage. She unrolled the tapestry across her bed. City streets lead upward to a castle with high towers. A foreign flag stood proudly on its pole. She could almost hear the bustle of crowds in the marketplace and smell the golden sunshine. An odd longing beat in her chest.

A trumpeting fanfare announced the arrival of the expected guests. Derylla froze for a moment beside her bed and then raced to the window.

Banners passed beneath the gate. Grand horses clomped in rhythm on the cobbled walkway. Then a line of carriages rumbled by. A troop of her father's soldiers broke from the end. One of the foreign riders followed them into the stable.

Someone knocking at her door turned her attention away from the visiting royalty.

"You are summoned, my lady." A servant bowed after she opened the door.

Trepidation built as she walked the familiar hallways. She arrived at the throne room much too quickly.

"I wish to speak to my betrothed alone." A single figure draped in fur coats stood before the king.

Derylla watched from the doorway of the largest room of the palace. What would the king do with such an odd request?

"That is not the way it is done."

"Please Sire, I am weary from many days of travel. Indulge me this one thing."

Derylla was shocked to see her father wave an attendant to open a meeting room. The prince beckoned her to follow as he entered. Holding herself stiff, she obeyed. She walked to a window and threw open the drapery. Light flooded the room. She heard the click of the door closing. "You insult my family with your actions, sir."

"I did not lie when I spoke of weariness. I do not have it in me for pomp and ceremony."

Her ears perked at the sound of his muffled voice. She could hear him remove the bulk of his outer garment.

"It will not do, Princess. You will have to turn around some time."

Her heart clamored to life at the sound of his voice. She whirled around.

"Nolan." She whispered his name, barely able to believe her eyes.

"Prince Valanon." He bowed.

"But how? Why?"

He stepped closer. "When I heard I was to be married, I chose to travel here to meet you. God allowed me to learn of the plot against you. But I am known to none. My warning would not have been heeded. I joined with the men and hoped I would be able to protect you from the worst of it."

"But you were captured. Why did you not reveal your true identity?"

"What proof did I have? I carried nothing with me. There was naught to do but trust God."

"And then the dragon happened."

"It would come for your family. I cherished your friendship and knew I would have to defeat the beast. And then you were too stubborn to go home, and I had to protect you myself."

"Protect me? Seems I recall finding you near death after Michaels stabbed you."

He smiled. "You had your own near-death experience."

They stood staring at one another, deeper emotions at play beneath the surface. Nolan took a step closer. Then another and another, until he could touch her cheek. "I would have died to protect you, to keep you from harm."

She smiled; joy barely able to describe the well of emotion awakening within her. "But then you would not be able to surprise me like this."

"Derylla," he said her name as a laugh.

She tugged him closer still, allowing his mouth to claim her own. His kiss curled her toes and love burst through her heart.

They returned hand in hand to the King's room.

"I accept Prince Valanon's offer." Derylla's voice resonated through the room. She never turned her eyes from him, and his smile washed all sorrows away.

Thank you for reading my second collection of fairytales. The next collection, *Thrice Upon a Time in Fairy Land*, will bring even more wonderful tales of magical realms, princes, princesses, and of course, faeries. Until then, here's a list of other stories by Laurie Lee to enjoy.

- Cinderella Spell
- Legends: Within the Dark Realm
- Once Upon a Time in Fairy Land

Laurie Lee is the fantasy penname for author Laurie Boulden. Enjoy these other selections by Laurie.

- Sisters of Mercy House Gardens: Lilly and that Nice Detective (suspense)
- Sisters of Mercy House Gardens: Astra and that Handsome Bachelor (contemporary romance)
- Hidden Gems (suspense)
- By the Fruit of Her Hands: Jewel of Jericho (Biblical fiction)
- By the Fruit of Her Hands: Mistress of Moab (Biblical fiction)

- By the Fruit of Her Hands: Pearl of Persia (Biblical fiction)
- By the Fruit of Her Hands: Journeying the Walls of Jericho (Biblical devotion)
- Cookies, Cocoa, and Capers (Christmas rom com)
- Her Christmas Misfortune (Christmas rom com)
- A Time to Die (time travel suspense)
- The Cat from Camden Place (suspense with a touch of fantasy)
- Cowboy Blessing (sweet romance)
- The Maxwell Murders (suspense)
- Flood: A Wife for Shem (Biblical Fiction)

Connect with author Laurie Boulden:

- On Facebook
- On Instagram
- On Twitter
- Website

It isn't quite a fairytale but enjoy this first chapter from The Cat from Camden Place. A little bit of mystery, a whole lot of kitty magic.

The first light of dawn dazzled the creek bubbling across rocks and pebbles in its ancient course. Mitchel Ryce sipped his coffee as he contemplated the passing water through the culvert directly behind his side of the duplex. Bird calls rose through the stand of trees surrounding the creek. The ring of the phone didn't break the gentle peace of morning. He watched a pair of squirrels chase each other through the old oak as he responded to the call. "Detective Ryce." Saying his new title stirred something within that the coffee could not.

"Captain's assigning you to a fresh scene. I'll send the address to your phone. You'll be on your own until Webber can get freed up from something on the south end of the county."

"Thank you, Pearl. I'm on my way." He gulped the last of the coffee before jumping to his feet. He already wore a suit along with his long beige wool-silk scarf—his choice for the first official day as a lead detective.

The drive across Camden Place took him from the duplexes on his own block to the smaller bungalows built in the last century when the local mines were strong. GPS announced his arrival, as if the flashing lights of several patrol cars didn't. He parked on the other side of the street.

With neighbors crowding close on the front

lawn, Ryce flashed his badge and pointed at the large pecan tree breaking up the sidewalk. "Set a perimeter, let's get them off the grass. Could be evidence being trampled underfoot."

"Yes, sir." The officer reached into his car for crime scene tape.

Ryce continued up four concrete steps to the front porch. A worn carpet with faded blue and gray flowers marked a seating area. The wicker settee and rocker had been repainted white more than once. A cup on the low table still had liquid in it. The front door led directly into a living room with a kitchen to the right. Two doors leading off the living room were open. Through one he saw a bed and the other was an office with a brown desk.

The victim lay on the floor of the living room. Her head twisted toward the kitchen, eyes open, one reddened by hemorrhaging. "Who is she?" he asked the officer standing uncomfortably nearby. The younger man handed Ryce an ID. "Lanie Smith?" Ryce looked from the ID to the woman on the floor. It was her. "What did you do to end up this way?"

He crouched beside the body. Nails on both hands were messy. She put up a fight. "Bag her hands. She's got DNA for us." He breathed. "That will be helpful, Lanie." The air in the house wasn't ripe. Strangulation happened sometime during the night. "Who found her?"

The officer pointed to the front yard. "Her neighbor came over for a morning coffee."

Ryce returned his attention to Lanie. She wasn't young, neither was she old and wrinkled. A scarf around her neck had fallen back, revealing the thick red lines of strangulation. He looked toward the door. A Paris-themed coat hook board had another scarf and a long leash. The victim wore a calf-length nightgown, not something you would wear with a scarf. Had the killer brought a scarf or borrowed what already hung near the door? Had he come unprepared? Ryce investigated the bedroom. Floral covers were pulled back, draping almost to the floor on the left side of the bed. Light in the bedroom came from the living room. Had someone knocked and she willingly got up from the bed? Had she been forced from it? He looked at the kitchen and considered the cup of something on the porch. Perhaps she'd been unable to sleep. A crime of passion?

The jumble of thought didn't disturb his focus. Movement from under the bed caught his attention. He narrowed his gaze. Yes, something moved. He couldn't tell what, but there was something beneath the bed.

Ryce motioned for the officer to stand on one side of the doorway into the bedroom. Making sure his weapon was obtainable, he took the right side. "Whoever is under the bed, come out now." Nothing moved. Ryce reached around to turn on the overhead light. The lamp on the bedside table had fallen over and a cell phone cord lay on the floor. No phone. An odd gurgling noise came from under the bed. Ryce looked at the other officer. "Ask the neighbor what kind of dog Lanie has."

But there wasn't a need. Two large paws came into view.

"I don't think I've ever seen dog paws that

fluffy," Ryce muttered. "I'm guessing you're not a dog."

The brief conversation seemed to have an impact. A head peaked, went back in, and then, in a burst of motion, something very large hurdled from beneath the bed, through the doorway, to jump onto the couch. The other officer staggered back, fighting to pull his gun from its holster. Ryce placed a hand on his arm. "Let's not shoot the cat."

The man shook his head. "That's no cat, it's too giant."

Ryce didn't disagree. The head of the cat was easily the size of his own head. Its ears were pulled back and fur around its neck and shoulders seemed thicker and bristled. The eyes of the cat were bright yellow around the almond-shaped pupils. A mesh of black, gray, brown, and white covered the face and body.

"Have the CS team check for fingerprints in the bedroom. Looks like she was pulled from the bed, let's hope her attacker left plenty of evidence behind."

"What about that thing?" The officer moved closer to the kitchen.

"Get animal control. Or maybe the neighbor will take it."

The cat's tail swished as it watched Ryce. Ryce explored the rest of the house. A door in the other bedroom led into the backyard. Glass on the floor revealed an unfriendly point of entry. The desk was a medium brown color, with gentle movement in its design. Wear on the edge of it, where Lanie would likely sit, seemed dimmer and scratched. There was a monitor on the desk, but no CPU. He searched a bookcase on the other wall of the room. A printer was untouched. A laptop cord lay beside it, but no sign of a laptop. He turned and jumped at the sight of the cat standing behind him. "I'm working," he assured the animal. "Haven't solved it yet." He glanced around but no one else was nearby. "This is my first case." The cat didn't seem perplexed.

The crime scene team didn't need him hanging around to micromanage, so he headed next door to their first witness. Mrs. Grisby was a little older and rounder than Lanie. "Good morning, ma'am. How are you holding up? Do you have family or a friend who can spend the day with you? Shouldn't be alone after the fright you had earlier."

"I just can't believe it." Mrs. Grisby motioned him to take a seat. "That poor woman. Such a nice lady. Don't understand why someone would do that."

"I ask myself that same question more frequently than I like. Do you remember hearing anything?"

She shook her head. "Once I take my ears out, it would require a blast from a bullhorn to get my attention. I'm sorry, dearie, I had no idea."

"Of course not. This is not on you. Have you noticed anything odd recently? Any changes or new people coming around?"

"Not really. The cat, of course. I think about a month or so ago. Nearly scared me out of my skin, never seen a cat that big before. She assures me it's normal. A Maine Coon."

"That recent? Did she have a name for it?"

"Calls her Whiskers. Called," Mrs. Grisby pressed a hand to her chest and blinked. "Called her Whiskers."

"I'm sorry for your loss. Did the officer talk to you about coming down to the station to get your statement?"

She nodded. "I don't drive anymore, so he said they'll send a car for me."

Ryce pulled a business card from his back pocket. "If you think of anything else, please give me a call."

Ryce studied the neighborhood as he walked back to his car. Having the area around the house taped off seemed to send most of the neighbors back to their houses. A pair of officers were going house to house. The coroner's sedan had arrived. The CS truck was onsite as well. Ryce pulled his jacket off and opened the passenger door. Before he could toss his jacket across the seat, the cat jumped into his vehicle. He jerked back, but the multi-colored Maine Coon sat on its haunches, tail curled around her feet, staring at him. "You're supposed to stay inside the house until someone comes for you." He frowned.

From somewhere behind, he heard chuckles. "Problem there, sir?"

Ryce sighed. "No, we're good." He glared at the cat but closed the passenger door.

Printed in Great Britain
by Amazon

62105809R00090